rk of a careful and conscientious writer . . . Vlautin, like
sical equivalents Tom Waits and Shane MacGowan, man-
render pathos without sentimentality in prose whose tone
nbeat, fatalistic and hangdog.' *Hot Press*

et and aching story . . . which has drawn comparisons in
nd voice to the work of Vlautin's hero Raymond Carver. His
is steeled with a disconcertingly pure honesty [but] the
cannot but grow to like and worry for the brothers' *Irish*

ll the best bits of Denis Johnson and Raymond Carver
up into something new and strange and funny.' *Nude*

nyself picking up *The Motel Life* and rereading it because
because it's got everything that great books should; it has
nd great writing and ambivalence and complexity and
and life . . . Other books published this year will have to
ways to better Vlautin's debut.' *Bookmunch.co.uk*

eld masterpiece . . . like his band, his book was a darkly
slice of Americana.'
Big Issue, Books of the Year ?

THE MOTEL LIFE

a novel

WILLY VLAUTIN

faber and faber

First published in 2006
by Faber and Faber Limited
Bloomsbury House, 74–77 Great Russell Street
London WC1B 3DA
This paperback edition published in 2007

Typeset by Faber and Faber Limited
Printed and bound by CPI Group (UK) Ltd, Croydon, CRO 4YY

A CIP record for this book
is available from the British Library

ISBN 978-0-571-22808-9

4 6 8 10 9 7 5

For Chuck Holt

I

THE NIGHT IT HAPPENED I was drunk, almost passed out, and I swear to God a bird came flying through my motel room window. It was maybe five degrees out and the bird, some sorta duck, was suddenly on my floor surrounded in glass. The window must have killed it. It would have scared me to death if I hadn't been so drunk. All I could do was get up, turn on the light, and throw it back out the window. It fell three stories and landed on the sidewalk below. I turned my electric blanket up to ten, got back in bed, and fell asleep.

A few hours later I woke again to my brother standing over me, crying uncontrollably. He had a key to my room. I could barely see straight and I knew then I was going to be sick. It was snowing out and the wind would flurry snow through the broken window and into my room. The streets were empty, frozen with ice.

He stood at the foot of the bed dressed in underwear, a black coat, and a pair of old work shoes. You could see the straps where the prosthetic foot connected to the remaining part of his calf. The thing is, my brother would never even wear shorts. He was too nervous about it, how it happened, the way he looked with a fake shin, with a fake calf and foot. He thought of himself as a real failure with only one leg. A cripple. His skin was blue. He had half-frozen spit on his chin and snot leaking from his nose.

'Frank,' he muttered, 'Frank, my life, I've ruined it.'

'What?' I said and tried to wake.

'Something happened.'

'What?'

'I'm freezing my ass off. You break the window?'

'No, a duck smashed into it.'

'You kidding?'

'I wouldn't joke about something like that.'

'Where's the duck then?'

'I threw it back out the window.'

'Why would you do that?'

'It gave me the creeps.'

'I don't even want to tell you, Frank. I don't even want to say it. I don't even want to say what happened.'

'You drunk?'

'Sorta.'

'Where are your clothes?'

'They're gone.'

I took the top blanket off my bed and gave it to him. He wrapped it around himself then plugged in the box heater and looked outside. He stuck his head out the broken window and looked down.

'I don't see a duck.'

'Someone probably stole it.'

He began crying again.

'What?' I said.

'You know Polly Flynn, right?'

'Sure.' I leaned over and grabbed a shirt on the floor and threw up into it.

'Jesus, you okay?'

'I don't know.'

'You want a glass of water?'

'No, I think I feel a little better now.' I lay back in bed and closed my eyes. The cold air felt good. I was sweating, but my stomach began to settle.

'I'm glad I don't puke at the sight of puke.'

'Me too,' I said and tried to smile. 'What happened?'

'Tonight she got mad at me,' he said in a voice as shaky as I've ever heard. 'I don't remember what I said, but she yelled at me so hard that I got up to get dressed but she got up first and took my pants and wouldn't give them back. She ran outside and set fire to them with lighter fluid. I had my wallet and keys in my coat, but the main thing, the real thing, is that I left. Got in my car and started driving home. I was a little drunk, but Jesus, I was okay to drive, and I was just going down Fifth Street, and some kid runs out in the middle of the road on his bike and I hit him. It's fucking four in the morning, there's snow on the ground, there's snow coming down. What's a kid doing riding his bike around at that time of night in that sorta weather? There were no other cars behind me, no one around at all to help. I wasn't even going twenty. There was no stop sign. I didn't run anything. It wasn't like that. He just came out of nowhere. I stopped as fast as I could. I got out to take a look, and the kid's there on the snow and asphalt with his head busted open and blood coming out of his mouth. Jesus, I didn't know what to do. I went back into the car where I got a blanket in the back seat, and I covered him with it. Used part of it to put over his head where the bleeding was. I think he was dead right then. I checked his breathing and pulse, but there was nothing. No one was around. Just the little light coming down off the street lights. By that thrift store, by that old RESCO warehouse. I didn't know what to do. I couldn't leave the kid there so I put him in the back seat, 'cause I was gonna bring him to the hospital. Then when I picked him up I knew for sure he was dead. Part of the inside of his head had come out. I'd never seen anything like it. It was the most horrible thing I ever saw.

'I began thinking of how I was drunk and how I'd go to jail. Jesus Christ. I put him in the back seat anyway, and I get in, and suddenly I see this taxi cab turn on his lights. He'd been in a vacant lot about a block away. Maybe he was sleeping, who knows. Maybe he saw the whole thing, but if he did he would have stopped, wouldn't he? He would have helped me? But he just drove off in the opposite direction. So I start driving to Saint Mary's, maybe ten minutes ago, but the kid's dead. Ain't much use in taking him in, is there? If I'd run a light or something, sure, but I didn't. He hit me more than I hit him. I don't know what the fuck to do. I had the right of way, I did, I swear I did.'

'What the hell are you talking about?' I said and sat up.

'I'm the worst person in the goddamn world.'

I got out of bed and put on my pants and shoes.

I looked out the window. His car was down there like he said.

4

The sky was half dark; there was new snow on the ground and some still falling. There were hardly any people on the street below. It was a hard thing to imagine a kid in the car like that.

Jerry Lee stood in front of the heater, the orange glow reflected on his body. He was shaking.

'You're not kidding?'

'No,' he said, 'that's the last thing in the world I'd kid about.'

'Why don't you get in bed? I got the electric blanket going.'

'Let me just stand here for a second then I will.'

I looked outside again. I saw a truck delivering newspapers to the casinos, I saw two taxis drive by.

Jerry Lee moved to my bed. His boots hung off the side.

'It's goddamn cold out,' he said.

I found my bathroom towel and covered the puke. Then I threw it all in a trash basket and stuck the basket in the hall. I got a glass of water from the sink, put on my parka, and sat in the recliner.

'Frank,' he said and began weeping, 'I don't understand how it could happen. You should have seen his face. He still looked alive when I went to him but, Jesus, he wasn't. He's so young. He probably ain't even in high school yet. I just don't understand why this is happening.'

He took the keys out of his coat pocket, and threw them at me. I set the keys on the floor.

'I can barely stand up,' I said.

'What'd you drink?'

'Doesn't matter. What you said, it really happened? You swear on your life?'

'It happened,' he said and turned away and began crying harder.

5

I stood up and got my shampoo and soap. 'I'm going to take a shower. I can barely stand my stomach hurts so bad. When I get back maybe I'll feel better and then we'll figure something out.'

2

I WALKED DOWN THE HALL and locked myself in the shower room. I sat there for a long time letting the hot water fall over me. I lay down and curled in a ball on the cool tile floor hoping it would ease the pain in my stomach and after a long while it did.

I walked back to my room wet and dried myself with a pair of jeans. I put on long underwear, pants, a long-sleeved flannel shirt, shoes, and my parka. I stood in front of the heater.

'Is that kid really in your car?' I asked.

Jerry Lee had the covers up to his neck.

'Yeah,' he said and tears began again. I hadn't seen him cry in years, maybe since we were kids. 'I don't know why it happened, but it did.'

'Why didn't you call the police or an ambulance?'

'Like I said, there was no one around, no phone booth, no store, nothing. I didn't know what to do so I just put him in the car and started driving towards the hospital. But then I knew he was already dead.'

'But you didn't do anything wrong, really, that's the main thing.'

'But I was drunk. I'd go to jail. They'd say I killed him.'

I went to my closet and gave Jerry Lee a pair of pants to wear. He dressed and we went down to the street below. I opened the car door, and in the dimness of the inside light I could see the kid. His face covered in a blanket. Worn-out jeans and faded black tennis shoes. Pale white arms bent in wrong directions. It was a horrible thing to see. I shut the door and we walked around for a while and tried to figure out what to do.

It was almost dawn when we drove a block from Saint Mary's Hospital and left the poor kid on the frozen grass in front of an office building. Jerry Lee carried him from the car telling him how sorry he was. Then we drove to the Cal Neva, parked in their lot, and started drinking. By nine, I was drunk again, and by ten we left the casino and walked to the bank.

We emptied both our accounts but I had only $234 in savings, and Jerry Lee had less than a hundred. While we were in line I kept thinking about the kid. Maybe he had been sleeping in the warm bed of his girlfriend an hour before he died. He might have snuck out her window when he knew he had to leave. Might have been laying there next to her, and she was naked and he's about to fall asleep; maybe it was then that he made himself get up and get dressed. Maybe he heard her mom get up and use the toilet. Maybe he kissed her before he left. Maybe he got back in bed with her one last time before he made himself go for sure. I hope it was like that, and not the other way. That he was running from something, or that he had nowhere to go, or that he couldn't go home 'cause things were so bad there.

Bad luck, it falls on people every day. It's one of the only certain truths. It's always on deck, it's always just waiting. The worst thing, the thing that scares me the most is that you never know who or when it's going to hit. But I knew then, that morning, when I saw the kid's frozen arms in the back of the car that bad luck had found my brother and me. And us, we took the bad luck and strapped it around our feet like concrete. We did the worst imaginable thing you could do. We ran away. We just got in his beat-up 1974 Dodge Fury and left.

3

THE FIRST THING WE DID was get a full tank of gas, and then we went to the store. We bought a twelve-pack of beer, a pint of Jim Beam, some ant-acid pills, a bottle of Pepto, three pre-made sandwiches, some cleaning products, a package of glazed donuts, and then we parked behind the Day's Inn on Seventh Street. We cleaned up the blood on the back seat with a roll of paper towels and a spray bottle of 409. We didn't go home and get our things. We didn't call anybody. I didn't call in at work.

'Where do you want to go?' I asked him as I pulled us out onto the road.

'To Montana,' Jerry Lee said and opened a beer.

'It's probably snowing up there.'

'At least it's out of state, less people than in California. We could take the car out in the middle of nowhere, in the woods. We could buy a bunch of gas and burn it. Stack it full of wood inside and set it on fire.'

'I guess,' I said but I wasn't really thinking. I knew I was about to be sick again. I pulled the car over to the side of the road and got out as fast as I could.

My brother rolled down the window after I was done and said, 'Jesus, Frank, you're a mess.'

'I can't help it,' I told him.

'You want me to drive?'

'Maybe,' I said and he got out of the car and I got in the passenger seat. Jerry Lee put us back on the road and got us on the highway. I opened a beer and turned on the radio and found the oldies country and western station.

'Head wherever you want,' I told him and closed my eyes. I leaned my face against the cold glass of the passenger side window.

'I'll just start east, then maybe take 95 up?'

'Okay,' I said.

We became quiet for a while, and I fell asleep for maybe an hour or so. When I woke I opened another beer and tried to eat a donut.

'You up?' my brother asked me and looked over.

'Yeah,' I told him.

'I'm sorry. I really am. I'm sorry for everything. I shouldn't have come by your room. I didn't know where else to go. I know I owe 300 bucks too. I just want to let you know that I'm damn sorry.'

'I don't care about the money.'

'I'm a goddamn horrible person.'

'No, you're not,' I said and looked out the window across the highway as we passed the town of Lovelock. They'd built a prison out there, and an Indian guy I'd worked with in the warehouses was supposedly there. That's what everyone said about him. Larry Jenkins is his name. It was just above freezing, but even still, in the distance I could make out people walking around in the yard, and I wondered if he was out there among them.

'You mind talking, Frank? When I'm alone with my thoughts all I think about is what happened.'

'What do you want to talk about?'

'Jesus, I don't care.'

'My stomach's getting worse,' I said.

'You should drink more milk.'

'I guess.'

'Or go see a doctor. They might have something you could take. You probably got an ulcer. You should stick to beer and drink Pepto with it.'

'That don't sound too good.'

'I've seen guys do it, but it looks pretty horrible to me too.'

'I read somewhere that the town of Lovelock is the home of some famous woman who was in Charlie Chaplin movies. She was Chaplin's girlfriend for a long time. He went through the women, but he always liked her. He supported her, I think. For her whole life he did.'

'Did she move back to Lovelock?'

'No, she lived in San Francisco.'

'She still alive?'

'No,' I said, 'she drank herself to death in the 1940s, I think.'

'That's not helping, I guess,' Jerry Lee said.

'What isn't?'

'You talking,' he said and laughed. He turned the stereo back up and so I stared out the window at the frozen desert and after a while fell asleep.

4

WE DROVE ALL THAT DAY without hardly stopping. We'd talk for a while, then we'd listen to the radio, every now and again we'd stop at a gas station if one passed our way. Both our moods were pretty dark. We couldn't stop thinking about the kid. For a time we were on Highway 80, and then we turned north on Highway 95 and drove until it got dark. By then we were near the Oregon border, near the small town of McDermitt. Jerry Lee pulled off the highway onto a dirt road and drove a mile or so on it and shut off the car. I went to the trunk and took out these two old sleeping bags he kept in there and got back in the car. Jerry Lee moved to the back seat and we got into the bags and tried to knock off.

We were quiet for a long time. I had the radio going to help me sleep, but the night was hard, and after a time I could hear Jerry Lee crying. It was real quiet, the way he cried, like he was whimpering. Like a sick dog might, or maybe a dying old man. I didn't say anything to him 'cause I didn't know what to say.

But that night even when I did get to sleep, it wouldn't last. The wind began to blow and it started snowing in flurries. I got worried about getting stuck, about cars passing us, or the police noticing us and thinking we were stranded or broken down.

I got so nervous after a while that I woke Jerry Lee. I yelled at him, but he just lay there in the back like he was dead. Finally I sat up and leaned over the seat and shook him until he woke.

'What do you want?' he said in the darkness.

'I can't sleep.'

'Jesus, why not? It's too fucking cold out to do anything else.'

'We should get back on the road.'

'Let's wait 'til morning.'

'You think so?' I asked.

'I'm too tired to drive and you can't see worth a shit at night,' Jerry Lee said and coughed.

'What station you been listening to?'

'It's out of Redding, California,' I said. 'It's a talk show about business or something.'

'It sounds boring as hell.'

'I ain't really listening.'

He sat up. 'Put on that Willie Nelson tape, will you? I hate when they talk on the radio. I got that song "Railroad Lady" stuck in my head again.'

I sat up and turned on the inside light. I found the tape, put it in, and turned the light back off.

'You think there's wolves out here?'

'No,' I said. 'There's a few mountain lions, I bet, but all the ranchers, they shot the wolves years ago.'

'What about coyotes?'

'I bet there's some.'

'Maybe we'll see them.'

'I hope so,' I said.

'I think the only thing that will get me back to sleep is beer.'

I reached over to the floorboards and took a beer from the sack and handed it back to him.

'I just started getting antsy,' I said. 'I felt like I had to wake you.'

'It's all right,' he said and opened the can. 'You know what I was thinking about just before I fell asleep?'

'What's that?'

'How when you started writing those letters to the horse track in Del Mar, the track near San Diego. How you wrote them asking if you and I could have jobs down there. That we'd work for free if they'd give us a room to live in. Dear Sir, we're only fifteen and seventeen and we've never seen a horse outside a parking lot, a rodeo, or a TV, but if you let us stay in a stall we'll work for free. You could feed us too if that's all right, or we could just eat at the concession stand. If you chose the concession stand we'll need a few bucks or some food vouchers or we can just eat the old hot dogs.'

Jerry Lee busted up laughing.

'Shit,' I said and sat up. 'How did you remember that?'

'Just came to me.'

'I wrote those assholes every week. Them and Santa Anita, but I figured if Del Mar took us, then we could go to the beach. Maybe learn how to surf or scuba dive.'

'Can you imagine if they would have written back? We'd be down in San Diego right now instead of out here in the boonies.'

'I should have lied a bit more,' I said, and in the darkness I was smiling. 'I wrote them all year long. Maybe something like forty letters.'

'The horse track, Jesus.'

'It wasn't that bad an idea,' I said.

'No, it was a good idea, it was a real great idea,' he said. His voice still light and easy. 'It was one of the best ideas I've ever heard.'

5

I WOKE THE NEXT MORNING and got sick out the driver's side window. The car was covered in snow and the wind was howling, blowing snow in flurries, and at times it was almost as bad as a white out.

'That ain't much of a wake-up call,' Jerry Lee said when he heard me.

'You got chains?' I asked him and laid back down on my sleeping bag.

'I don't know,' he said. 'Jesus, it's snowing. Holy hell. If I do they'd probably be in the trunk, but I don't drive when it snows so I don't know for sure.'

'I hate driving at all,' I said.

'When it starts falling,' Jerry Lee said, 'I walk. I don't trust people, you'd be crazy to. Most don't know how to drive, and then you add snow and it's a goddamn mess. If it snowed all the time, say like you're in Michigan or Alaska, then it'd be different. I guess I'd trust people then. But it doesn't. Ice is worse. I just stay home if there's ice. I won't even walk on the sidewalk.'

I started the Dodge and turned the heater on. I set my pants next to the floor vent, and put them on when they had warmed. Then I put on my shoes and my coat and got out and wiped the snow off the windows. We were parked on top of a hill overlooking a valley. I checked the trunk and there were no chains, nor a jack or even a tire iron. I walked down the road a while to see how it was, and the snow was deep, maybe a foot. I wasn't sure we could get back to the highway even if we had chains.

For a time I ate snow and looked down into a gully. The cool air and the snow helped calm my stomach, and all around me the snow was new and untouched, with no tracks coming or going. As I stared off I saw a deer appear maybe a half a mile away on the top of another ridge. I'd never seen one in the wild before. I've seen them dead on the highway, and on TV, but never like that.

As it got closer I could see it didn't have any horns and it was really quite small, maybe it was just a young one or baby. It began running down a gully about a hundred yards from where I was. It was quick and ran effortlessly, and just seeing it seemed to ease my mind in a way I didn't understand. I watched it for a long while until it turned up a hill and finally disappeared into the distance.

I walked back to the car and got in.

'The woods could be all right for us,' I told him. I found a pre-made turkey sandwich and began trying to eat it.

'I don't know,' he said from his sleeping bag. His voice was raw and cracked and I could tell he'd been crying again.

'Maybe we should move out to the woods. Rent a cabin or something. Nothing weird happens out here. Nothing like a kid getting hit by a car.'

Jerry Lee sat up. He found a beer at his feet and opened it. 'Jesus, I don't want to think about that, not right now. Don't bring it up. And about the woods, there's nothing to do out here, and what's worse is all those kids that get their arms chopped off in farm machinery. They end up driving around town with their feet. Trees fall on people, chain saws and things like that. Horrible things happen in the woods, believe me. How about those families that get murdered out in the woods? Bears, rodents, snakes, and more bugs than anywhere else in the world, crazed Vietnam vets, hillbillies.'

'It ain't like that,' I said.

'Maybe, maybe not,' he said and coughed. 'You mind putting in that Willie Nelson tape?'

'We been listening to it all night.'

'We got to do something,' he said.

I put the tape back in and turned the sound down low.

'What's different about the woods is that there's no people.'

'You got a point there,' Jerry Lee said. 'But let's get the hell out of here anyway. You might like it, but it's starting to give me the fucking creeps.'

'I got to sit here for a while before I do anything,' I told him and closed my eyes.

'You know what I was thinking about last night? I was thinking about when we lived at the Sandman,' I said a while later, after my stomach had settled.

20

'Oh hell,' Jerry Lee said and sighed. 'That place was horrible. That was the second place we stayed at, wasn't it?'

'It was the third,' I said and looked out the window. I saw a small black bird trying to fly in the wind all alone. It was a strange sight seeing it out there in the middle of a storm surrounded by the white of the snow.

'Man,' Jerry Lee said, 'with that couple next door, yelling and screaming all the time, and then they'd just fuck, and you'd hear them night after night banging against the wall. And that drunk Indian from Fallon who would beat on our door in the middle of the night thinking it was his room. "Where's my fucking key, who's got my fucking key!" And the fucking smell of that place. I hated the smell of that place. I hated that place more than anything or anywhere.'

'At least the Indian bought us beer.'

'Yeah, that's something, I guess, but I hated it all the same. Having to go to work at that warehouse and then come home to that. It was my first job after the Connelly brothers.' Jerry Lee sat up again. 'Jesus, Frank, I can't keep talking like this or I'm gonna kill myself. Let's just get out of here, maybe go find a place to eat some breakfast. Bacon and eggs or French toast. Even a waffle and coffee would do.'

I put the car in reverse and eased us backwards down the snow-covered dirt road. I was too uncertain to stop or turn around. The wheels spun some, but the snow was dry and somehow there was enough traction to keep us going.

'I knew we'd make it,' Jerry Lee said and smiled when I put us on Highway 95.

'I didn't think we would.'

21

'I couldn't see us getting stuck. When I pictured it in my mind it didn't fit. We ain't gonna get caught up that easy. It'll be something else, but it won't be like this.'

6

'IT WAS LIKE THAT, Frank, I swear it was. Just like that, out the blue. Out of nowhere. Everything was fine, I knew what I was doing. I was scared about the snow so I was barely going twenty and then the next second everything goes to hell. If Polly Flynn hadn't burned my pants, I probably would have stayed the night with her. If she hadn't burned my pants we wouldn't be here. Can you imagine that? Just her burning those pants killed a kid. Jesus, I hope they found him all right.'

'Someone found him.'

'Why couldn't it have been that the kid hit me? I ain't shit, maybe he was gonna be somebody.'

'I don't know.'

'I sure wish we had some Copenhagen,' Jerry Lee said. 'It always helps calm my nerves.'

'I haven't had a chew in almost a year.'

'I still do sometimes when I'm drawing. I can chew all day and watch TV and draw.'

'The only time I liked chewing was when I'd take a walk. At night. Walking through alleys or neighborhoods and chewing. Looking at all the houses and the people inside.'

'Remember Larry Gardner?'

'Yeah, that kid could chew a pack of Redman a day,' I said.

'He was like Clint Eastwood in that western.'

'*Outlaw Josie Wales*?'

'Yeah, that one. That guy could really chew,' Jerry Lee said and took a drink from his beer. 'He could do anything with it. But a guy like that, Clint, I mean, he's got to look after his teeth. Movie stars they don't do any of that shit. They got personal trainers teaching them how to chew, how to drive a car. Shit like that. Larry Gardner he's the one that's got that fucked-up arm, doesn't he?'

'Yeah, it's short,' I told him. 'They got a name for it, but I can't remember it. It's like you took a kid's arm, a kid maybe three years old, and you put it on a man, a full-grown guy.'

'Be hard to get by like that, I bet.'

'It would be,' I said. 'I saw him not too long ago and he looked like hell. Saw him at the Bonanza. He worked in a warehouse. It was ten o'clock in the morning. He was drunk and smelled like he had slept in his clothes for a month. He said his shift started in an hour.'

'Shit, that's rough.'

'I felt bad for him.'

'Maybe we could be truck drivers.'

'I wouldn't mind that.'

'We could just stay on the road and never stop. They got those trucks with beds in them. They have them with TVs and fridges. And truck stops are like little cities now. They have them with movie theaters and barbershops and showers. You could just stay on the road and in truck stops. You wouldn't have to live anywhere at all.'

7

THAT AFTERNOON WORE ON SLOWLY, and besides the occasional ranch, there was nothing but sagebrush and barren hills around us. Sometimes we'd go ten or twenty minutes without seeing another car. I had the old Dodge up to eighty and Jerry Lee got drunk and we fell into long spells of silence.

As evening neared we started talking more and listening to the radio. We spoke about our father and how he himself had tried to get us all to leave town one night. The story was one our mother had told us, and although I remember little of it, Jerry Lee said he remembered it pretty well.

I was young, maybe just five or so, when he came home in the middle of the night and woke our mother. He was frantic and loud and Jerry Lee turned on the small bedside light that sat between our two beds on an old milk crate and we listened.

'What do you mean they have the car?' she said.

'They just do.'

'We have the title,' she added. 'They can't just take the car. We paid for it.'

'I gave them the title, I had to.'

'Jesus Christ, Jimmy,' she said and began crying. 'If they have the car then why do we have to leave? It's the only thing we have. Isn't that enough?'

'No,' he said, 'it's worse than that. I'm still down over $8,000. The last few months have been killing me. I can't live here anymore. I'll kill myself if I do.'

'We can't just leave. All our things are here. Jerry Lee's about to start school.'

'Just pack your bags,' he said and walked down the hall and opened our bedroom door.

'We're going on vacation tonight,' he said and tried to smile. When you looked at him he looked a lot like my brother and me do today. Tall and thin with black hair and sad, hollowed-out blue eyes. He was a mechanic and even though it was the middle of the night he wore his gray work uniform. His hands were the only real distinguishing thing about his appearance. They were scarred and rough and bent from years of working on cars. He was always embarrassed by them. He'd worked full time since he was fifteen. First as a parts puller for an auto wrecker and then a few years later as a mechanic. He'd never done anything else.

'Just put some clothes in a bag. I know it doesn't make sense, but you got to do as I say. Be dressed and ready in a half-hour, and no talking. We got to be quiet,' he said and left the room.

By the time the cab came we were all sitting outside in the driveway of our small house. My mother sat on her suitcase and my father stood there, trying not to pay attention to her. The driver and my father loaded our things into the trunk and we drove to the Greyhound bus station.

We stood in the rundown lobby surrounded by our luggage and my father talked to her about where to go. He began listing places to her in the most optimistic way he could.

'What are we doing here?' she said finally and stood up to him. 'We can't just leave, what's that do for anyone? Can't we just straighten everything out? I'll meet with whoever you owe money to. I'll set up a payment schedule and pay them myself.'

'I don't know,' he said and shook his head.

'Where are we gonna get money to leave on? I cut up the new credit card and we're overdue on the rest.'

'I have money,' he said and took his wallet from his pants and showed her. 'I borrowed it from Ray Porter.'

'I'm not using Ray Porter's money,' she said. 'Look, Jimmy, what kind of people are we if we just run? Really, what kind? We'll get you help, we will, and we'll pay everyone off. You just got to stop gambling. If we're gonna make it you have to. We'll get you some help.' She went to him and put her arms around him.

'Look,' she said, 'the diner here is open, let's just go in and eat breakfast and talk about it. We'll figure out what to do. We don't have to just get on a bus. We don't just have to run out like criminals.'

She then picked up her bag and led us to the small diner. My father stood there and watched us slowly make our way across the lobby before he finally picked up his suitcase and followed.

We all ate breakfast there at that diner and by the end my mother had my father smiling and talking and eventually we took a cab back to our house. It was just past dawn when we arrived and my father laid down on the couch for a quick nap while my mother began to get ready for work.

That night in the bus station lay heavy on us as we drove down the highway. Neither of us said it, but we were both wishing we could have left that night, that if we had, then maybe everything would have been different, maybe we would have been different.

Wilson Dunlap

8

WE PULLED OVER in an abandoned campground later that night. The entrance had been plowed so we drove as far as we could, stopped where the road ended and the snow began, and slept in the car. In the morning we drove to a town called Council and bought gas and chains. The chains were over fifty dollars.

It was snowing again by then, falling down hard, so I put them on in front of the gas station, and when I got us going I had to slow down to ten miles an hour. I couldn't see much of anything at all.

We made it to Riggens by five p.m. and decided we'd have to stop for the night. The weather was still going, and although we now had the chains, we didn't want to risk the chance of going off the road and having to get the police or a tow truck to get us out.

They had a store there that was open and we bought some beer and a loaf of bread and some lunchmeat. We pulled the car behind a closed auto shop and waited. There was no one around. I could barely see across the street it was snowing so much. Jerry Lee was in the back seat and I was in the front.

'I think we're getting close to running out of money,' Jerry Lee said.

'We still got over $150. I got fifty or so in my pocket, and there's a hundred in the glove box.'

'I don't know what to do.'

I looked at him in the rear view. 'I don't know if you should go back home.'

'You think I should stay away?'

'Maybe.'

'Where would I go?'

'I don't know.'

'I've never really been anywhere.'

'Me neither.'

'I guess I could go to Hawaii.'

'Yeah.'

'Lay on the beach and eat bananas and coconuts.'

'Sounds all right,' I said.

'You know he didn't even have a coat on. There it was snowing and I wasn't wearing any pants and he wasn't wearing a coat. Why wouldn't he have had a coat on? That's weird, isn't it? Riding a bike in the goddamn snow with no coat on? You think it hurt him?'

'You mean with the car?'

'Yeah.'

'I don't know. If it did, it didn't hurt long.'

'I don't know why I put him in the car. It was just instinct, I guess. I just wish it would have happened with people around.

Maybe someone would have known what to do. I feel horrible about the kid, I really do. They'll send me to prison now.'

'Don't say that.'

'You remember Wilson Dunlap?'

'I don't think so,' I said.

'Wilson was the guy growing pot plants in his basement. I can't remember how many he had exactly, but he had a lot. He had the lights, a humidity machine, and that special nature music always playing. He was a hell of a nice guy. We used to sit around his basement, just him and me, smoke weed and talk to his plants. It was more like a science project. Biology or something. I really liked that part of it, 'cause it didn't seem like he was doing something against the law. I mean, we were growing things, from just seeds. That's crazy, isn't it? But the plants, something happened to them and they wouldn't get any bigger. A lot of them started turning brown, wilting. He got so depressed about it I thought he'd kill himself. Seriously. He was strange that way. Then he began asking people what they thought was wrong. He got drunk one night and told a guy that he'd met in the bar about it. The guy said it had to do with lighting, that he'd had the same problem himself. So Wilson takes the guy to his house. The guy was an undercover cop, and Wilson got three years in Carson City.

'I couldn't believe it. His girlfriend said he would probably get out in one and a half, but still that's almost two years. He didn't hurt anybody. He just sat around with his plants and worked at a video store. I remember I saw his girlfriend one night, I forget where we were, but she asked me if I would go visit him. I didn't want to, hell I really didn't, but I took a day off and she drove me out there. I almost didn't go in. I started thinking crazy thoughts.

Maybe they'd end up throwing me in there. I don't know, maybe somehow they'd find something out about me. Anyway, I sat in the lot debating it, and finally I said to myself, "If I was in there I sure hope he'd be there visiting me." And then I went in through the gates and did it.

'Now he'd only been in there a month or two. And when I saw him, he started crying. Not just tears, but sobbing. Like a child. He told me he didn't know if he could take it. He told me he wished he was dead. Each night, he said, he prayed that he wouldn't wake in the morning.

'I talked to him for a while, but I didn't know what to say. That was the only time I went. I guess I ain't much of a friend, but I couldn't take it after that. I just couldn't. When he got out I went to see him at his mom's place, but he was different. I don't know how he changed, but he did. Maybe he was just colder, more reserved. It's hard to explain. I don't know if I could take it.'

'Maybe I'm wrong,' I said after a time. 'Maybe we just get rid of the car somehow and head back to Reno. Maybe no one will know anything. It wasn't your fault some stupid kid couldn't ride a bike.'

'I don't know,' he said. 'Just seems like more than that somehow.' He began crying.

I turned on the inside light and looked around at him. He was sitting there with his hat down to his eyes and a pocket knife in his hand, pressing into the palm of his other hand. Blood was there leaking all over his hand and dripping down on the floorboards.

'What the hell are you doing?' I said and turned back around and shut off the light.

'I don't know,' he said.

I began getting jittery.

'You're gonna have to stop crying. We got to figure out what we're gonna do about it.'

I took two beers out of the grocery sack, opened one for myself, and gave him one.

'I fell deep this time, didn't I, Frank?'

'I think so,' I said. 'But we'll figure it out. We have to. I mean, first off, what do you do with a car like this? I mean, it's got numbers. Maybe someone is looking for the car, who knows? If someone saw you hit that kid, if that taxi did, then they'll know it was you, and it'll look bad that we left town.'

'Jesus, Frank, I don't know why we left.'

'We shouldn't have,' I said.

'You know, they tattooed a Hitler sign on Wilson Dunlap. His girlfriend was half Jewish. He didn't hate anyone. He said he had to. They made him. A bunch of guys in prison did. 'Cause you have to side with someone, you know? Jesus, I don't want Hitler tattooed on me.'

I looked out the window. There was a restaurant across the street. From the car I could just make out that there were people inside.

'Let's go get something to eat at that diner.'

'I don't know,' Jerry Lee said, 'I don't feel like being around anyone. You go. I don't think I can eat anyway. I'm gonna just sit here.'

So I finished my beer, put on my hat, zipped up my coat, and got out of the car.

With the snow coming down, the street lights lit up the main road like it was almost day, it was so bright out. As I walked across the street I saw an old man and woman playing cards in the camper of their truck. They were parked outside the diner. Then I heard somebody honk, and I knew without looking who it was. I turned and saw Jerry Lee slowly driving the Dodge out of town. I stood there and watched until the tail lights just flickered into nothing.

9

AFTER STANDING THERE for a while, looking down the road, I
went to where we were parked to see if he had left my things.
There were food wrappers, a nearly empty Jim Beam bottle laying
on the ground, but also my sleeping bag and a six-pack of beer.

I put my things in the covered doorway of the auto body shop
and went across the street and into the restaurant.

There was a wood stove burning in the center of the room, and
there were deer heads on the wall, and a stuffed rattlesnake
curled with its head raised and its fangs out resting on top of the
cigarette machine.

I sat at the counter and kept looking out the window expecting
to see Jerry Lee, but each time I looked back there was nothing,
just the falling snow and the street lights in the distance.

The waitress poured me coffee and gave me a menu. She was
smiling and talking to the other people at the counter. She wore an

old metal brace on her right leg, which made her limp. I could see the cook: he was an older man, overweight, smoking cigarettes in the back. After she gave me coffee I looked in my wallet and saw I had only sixty-seven dollars left.

I asked her if they had a bus that went through. She coughed and said there was a bus, Greyhound, but that it wouldn't be coming through town until tomorrow afternoon.

'That is if it can make it,' she said. 'This snow doesn't look like it'll let up. Maybe, but maybe not. You never can tell. I don't trust forecasts anymore. They plow, but you'll just have to see.'

'Where do I pick it up?'

'Right here when it comes. We open at seven. The bus, if it shows, will be here anywhere from two on.'

'You know how much it is?'

'It's twenty-two dollars fifty to Boise, anywhere else I don't know. You can call them from the payphone in the back. It's next to the bathroom.'

I got up and went to the phone and looked up the number for Greyhound and called them. The fare to Reno was sixty-one dollars seventy-five. That only left me with around seven dollars.

I ordered toast and milk to help my stomach, and listened to the radio they had playing until the restaurant closed two hours later.

When I left I began walking around the small town, but there wasn't much to see and my feet began to freeze, so I picked up my things and looked for somewhere to sleep.

I found a small grocery store that was closed down. There was a For Sale sign in the window. It had once been a filling station

37

and had a huge overhang, and I stopped underneath that, got in my sleeping bag, and waited for morning.

The snow stopped during the night. I got up once to take a leak and I checked the road and it didn't look too bad. I went back to sleep and when I woke the next time, there were no clouds and the sun was coming up. I got out of my sleeping bag, got dressed, and began walking around to warm up.

The same lady who closed the restaurant drove up in an old white Ford pick-up. She opened the restaurant, and let me in.

'You been walking around all night?'

'Kind of. I had a sleeping bag.'

'It's a good thing you didn't freeze,' she said. 'You know how to start a fire?'

'Yeah,' I said.

'Well, you get the wood stove burning, bring in some wood from the back, and I'll cook you breakfast.'

I thanked her and followed her in.

I got the fire going okay and when I stacked enough wood she cooked me a ham and cheese omelet, hash browns, and toast. The food tasted better than any I could remember. The morning customers began arriving, and I sat at the end of the counter and ate by myself. When I was done I drank hot chocolate and waited. Every time the waitress would pass by I thanked her and pretty soon she made a joke of it that I did. I got her address and told myself I'd pay her back when I had the dough. Maybe I'd get her some sort of gift or at least send her a postcard.

Once in a while I'd look out the window for the Dodge and Jerry Lee, but each time I saw a car go by, or a customer arrive, my heart fell as it was never him.

My mind started to drift and I began thinking about Annie James, which I hated, but they just kind of fell on me, my memories of her did. She was the only girlfriend I'd ever had, and the only girl besides a prostitute I'd been with. For a while she and her mom lived three doors down from me and Jerry Lee at the Sutro Motel on Fourth Street.

Her mother was an on-and-off-again prostitute who had been fired from most of the local brothels for drinking, drugs, things like that. She'd stay up for days at a time as she liked speed. Annie told me stories about her. There were a lot of fucked-up ones, she told me, but I'd also seen it with my own eyes.

Annie James and I met in the parking lot of that motel, and once we got to know each other she would stay some nights with me and Jerry Lee in our room. I was eighteen then. She was seventeen. She went to high school and tried hard at it. When Jerry Lee and I'd be watching TV in the evening, she'd just sit there on the bed reading or doing her homework. She was like that, worked hard. She didn't have a temper either, she wasn't mean like her mom. Her mom had an edge most of the time where you never knew what would happen or what she'd say. Sometimes she'd be nice, polite, and then an hour later, maybe less, you'd hear her yelling from three doors away like a crazed maniac.

Annie James is blonde, skinny, with dark blue eyes. When I knew her, she kept her hair back in a ponytail. She was funny too, said funny things, and she had a good smile.

The memory that came to me while I was sitting there in that diner was of a night when she was still in high school and she was spending the night at our room at the Mizpah.

39

She came over late and me and Jerry Lee were in bed watching TV. She didn't say much and just sat on the bed and soon after I fell asleep. The next time I woke it was the middle of the night and she was laying on her back listening to a small radio I kept by my bed.

'Did I wake you?' she asked.

'Can't you sleep?'

'No,' she said and I got up and went to turn on the small lamp I had on my dresser.

'Please don't turn on the light,' she said.

'It's all right, Jerry Lee can sleep through anything.'

In the dim light I could see her in her underwear and bra. Her left arm was turned palm up with a pillow under it and I could see three marks running horizontally across the inside of her arm.

'What happened?' I said.

'I burned myself with my curling iron.'

I moved closer to her and looked at them. They were dark red with patches of white from blistering.

'You don't curl your hair,' I told her.

'Sometimes I do,' she said.

'Jesus,' I said, 'you don't have to stay there. You can stay with me. She's crazy.'

'I want to leave,' she said. 'But you don't mean it, do you?'

'You can stay here for good if you want.'

'I might have to,' she said finally and tried to keep herself from crying. 'Are you sure it would be okay?'

'I am,' I said.

'You think Jerry Lee would mind?'

'I'll ask him but I don't think so,' I said. 'He likes you. We could get your things tomorrow.'

40

'Let me think about how to do it without her going nuts,' she said. 'I'll figure it out, okay?'

'All right,' I said. 'Does it hurt bad?'

'I put some burn cream on that I got from the drug store and that helps.'

'We could go get breakfast if you're hungry,' I said.

'I'd like to but it hurts too much to put on a shirt. I know what you could do, you could tell me a story like the ones you tell Jerry Lee.'

'What do you want it to be about?'

She was silent for a time then said, 'Maybe it could be you and me on an island in the middle of the Pacific Ocean. With the sun and we could go swimming all day long and sleep on the beach. But like in James Bond, you know? Like the one where he's on that island. The one we saw the other night. If you could, you could make us like that.'

'*Goldfinger?*' I said.

'Maybe. We watched a whole bunch of them, it was a marathon, don't you remember?'

'Yeah,' I said.

'Will you tell me one?'

'I'll try,' I said and turned off the light and lay next to her on the bed.

'One morning, and it was a cold one too, we went down this deserted road towards town. I was walking you to school. We were eating donuts and I was drinking coffee. You were drinking hot chocolate, 'cause you don't like coffee. Even soaked in sugar and milk you don't. So we walk towards downtown to where you could catch the bus, but all of a sudden a car pulls up. A big black

Cadillac with tinted windows, and these two big guys come out, and they're really strong and they grab us. One guy gets you, one guy gets me, and they put us in the car. Luckily we still had our donuts and our drinks because they drove us all the way to San Francisco without stopping. We asked them what was going on, but they wouldn't speak to us. We were both really scared. But it was warm in the car and we just sat there waiting.

'Well, they took us into a warehouse on some pier. Then they separated you and me. We were yelling for each other. "Annie," I yelled. "Annie, I'll find you," I said. "Wait for me, Frank," you said. "Don't give up hope!" Then they took me to this room and made me change clothes. They gave me an orange jumpsuit and I put it on. They put a chain around my neck that had a small tag with the number fifteen on it. The chain I couldn't get off, it was that tight, they had permanently locked it on. Then this guy came, like a doctor, and he said, "Fifteen, roll up your sleeves." And so I did. He took a blood sample, then he took my temperature, checked my heart, all that sorta thing, and then they led me onto this yacht, and that's when I saw you again. You were dressed in the same orange jumpsuit and your number was sixteen. The boat was huge, but it wasn't like a ship, like a naval boat or anything, and it wasn't as big as a cruise ship, it was just a big yacht. A boat for rich people. Well, this other guy, who was Number Four, told us to follow him. So we did, we didn't know what else to do. We went below deck and then you could hear the ship moving and we left San Francisco. They stuck me in the kitchen. As a cook's assistant. The fat-ass cook, he was Number Seven. You were stuck in house cleaning, with a lady, an old mean bag, Number Ten. No one said anything. I asked and asked Number Seven about you, and each time I did the chain around my neck would shock me, and let me tell you it hurt like hell. So we'd cook, bake, fry, cut and chop. That's all I did. For eight hours, maybe twelve hours, that first day. We made some great stuff, though. Soups and casseroles, Chinese food, Mexican, even pies. I made Number Seven make a few peach pies 'cause I know it's your favorite. We even had a prime rib cooking, and it was twice as good as at the Fitz. That night, after shift, they took me to a room and threw me in. It was dark inside and when I found a light, I turned it on, and there you were laying on the bed. It was a nice bed too. A queen size with good sheets and a warm blanket. There was a big window and if you looked out you could see the moon and the stars and the rolling sea. We lay in bed together, and you said, "I hate cleaning, but everything is clean already so we quit early. Number Ten, at first she was a mean old bag, but then we started playing cribbage, and then we ate this great prime rib dinner. They even had peach pie."

'So the next day came and the next day went, and it was like that for a long time, for weeks, for months. Then one evening there was a terrible storm out, and Number Seven was worried as hell and told me that we were gonna just make sandwiches, that he was too scared to cook. So I chopped up carrot and celery sticks while he made them. "We're so damn close to our destination we can't sink, can we?" he would say as sweat poured down his face. I didn't know what to think, so I went into the fridge and took out the last peach pie and I set it on a tray, and then I made a thermos of coffee, got a few Cokes, and a couple cold turkey sandwiches and I told him I was gonna head back to the room and wait it out. When I got there, you were sitting at the table looking out at the rough sea. I set the food down, and we ate lunch and watched. Then we got sleepy and took a nap but when we woke, it was to lightning. The loudest lightning you've ever heard, and after a while the ship got hit. "Holy shit," you said and we got dressed and went out to see what was going on. It was crazy, we saw the old man, Number One, he was in a gold wheelchair. He had a metal eye, and his hands were just hooks. "Looks like we're done," is all he said and then the speedboat that was hanging on a crane broke free and fell on him. I told you to hold on and I went below, and I filled a bag full of food and water. Hell, I took a whole prime rib and three pies and a ton of other stuff then I came back to where you were, and suddenly you were wearing a bikini.'

'I was wearing a bikini?'

'And you looked great.'

'What color was it?'

'Black.'

'I like black,' she said.

'I know,' I said.

She giggled.

'We have to be quiet,' I said, 'or Number Seventeen will wake up.'

'I'm sorry,' she said.

'It's okay, Sixteen,' I said in a whisper and continued. 'So I throw the food into the speedboat, which was still sitting on top of Number One, and then we both get in and wait until the ship sinks and the speedboat's free and we head off to this island which we can just make out through the rain and darkness. The storm's rough, I mean ten-foot waves, but I handle it okay, and soon, just as the sun's coming up the storm eases and we head into this beautiful bay and we stop at this dock and you jump out in your bikini and tie up the boat. I get out with all the food and we walk up to this large mansion sitting on this bluff overlooking the sea and a huge beach. No one is inside, just us. There's electricity and we walk around. There's a jacuzzi inside with a slide, a huge movie room, and an ice skating rink, which is good 'cause I know how you like to ice skate. We sit on this huge deck and they have a telescope and we try to find our crew, but no one's in sight. We move a bed out to the deck and we just lay out on it and watch the waves crashing the beach. "I guess we'll stay here for a while," I said. "I guess so," you said. The End.'

'I wish that were true,' she said. 'I wish more than anything in the world that was true.'

'It is,' I said. 'It just ain't happened yet.'

I was at the counter staring off like that when the lady came up to me and gave me a western novel called *Lonesome Dove*. She said she thought it might pass the time, and so I spent the rest of the day getting wood, shoveling, eating, and trying to read that book, which turned out to be a pretty good one.

Around dusk the bus showed up. It was three hours late and by that time it was snowing again. I bought my ticket and sat in the back, near a window, and fell asleep. Hours later I got off in Boise. I had just enough money for a ticket to Reno.

ST MARYS HOSPITAL

10

WHEN I GOT HOME I didn't do anything but sit in my room and watch TV. I didn't call anybody, not even work. I just lay in bed and waited for Jerry Lee, hoping that he was okay, hoping that he'd come home.

On the third day Polly Flynn, the girl who burned Jerry Lee's pants that night, came to my room. I opened the door in my underwear and a ski cap.

She entered wearing skin-tight jeans, a light green parka, white earmuffs, and leather boots.

'What happened to the window?' was the first thing she said and walked over to it and looked out.

'A duck,' I said.

'What do you mean?'

'A duck flew into the window.'

'You're not funny. Just get some clothes on.'

I closed the door behind her and got back in bed. She sat in the chair I have by the window and began crying.

'The reason I came,' she said finally, 'is that Jerry Lee shot himself last night. Didn't you know? Hadn't you heard? He shot himself in his bad leg. They might have to amputate the rest of it. Isn't that just the most horrible thing you've ever heard?'

I got out of bed, put on my clothes, took the last of the reserve money I'd hid in my work boots, and we left.

While she drove us there she said Jerry Lee had told her that he had tried to kill himself, but that he didn't have the nerve to shoot himself in the head and decided to shoot himself in the thigh and bleed to death. He'd come by her house yesterday and asked to borrow her car. She gave him the keys and he left. He didn't say where he was going or what he was doing. Then he drove to Horsemen's Park, shut off the engine, turned up the radio, pulled out the gun, pointed it at his head, then at his leg, and fired. Turned out the park he chose was near a firehouse. The firemen heard the shot and called the police.

When the police found him, he was unconscious and bleeding heavily out of his right thigh. He had a loaded .357 in the seat next to him. The fire department then came, put a tourniquet on his leg, wrapped it in a bandage, and called for an ambulance.

She parked the car in the lot at Saint Mary's Hospital and we walked in the side entrance and took an elevator up to the third floor where Jerry Lee lay in intensive care. He had an IV in his arm, all sorts of wires coming from his hands, and a tube in his nose. There were a few machines gauging things. His bed sat near the window and he was awake.

Polly Flynn began crying.

Nurses kept coming in and out, making me nervous. There were other patients in the room, two of them. Old men, alone and watching TV.

Jerry Lee wouldn't say anything much. He just stared at the TV. Nobody said anything and the whole time you could hear the sound of Polly Flynn crying. Everyone began staring at us.

'Look,' I finally said to her, 'would you mind leaving us alone for a bit? I got a couple things I want to say.'

She took a Kleenex from her purse and wiped her eyes. She stood up.

'You heal up, kid,' she said and kissed him on the forehead. 'I'll be back. Don't you worry about a thing.'

He smiled at her and then she walked out of the room.

I pulled up a chair and said as softly as I could, 'What the fuck were you thinking?'

He remained silent for a time then said, 'Why should I live if that kid doesn't get to? There ain't no reason, is there? I'm a loser, Frank, and I know it, and I don't want to talk about it right now. I'm too tired. Could you just find us something on TV?'

I took the remote control and began switching channels back and forth. I found a movie and left it on that. He showed me his leg and said a few things about the operation. He looked awful, all sweaty and pale.

I stayed there all day, but he was asleep most of the time. When I left I bought a six-pack of beer at the first mini-mart I came across and walked to a dollar movie house. I snuck the beer underneath my coat, and sat in the back drinking and watching this movie about a waitress and a busboy. It was a love story. I'd seen the movie a couple times before. I knew all the words and the shocks and when everybody was supposed to cry. I knew when the bad parts would happen, and I knew I could just go to the bathroom during those parts and make it back to the parts that weren't so bad, and the parts that were good. But when it got real bad for the last time, and the guy in the movie was ready to die, I finished my last beer, put on my coat and hat, and left.

II

I DIDN'T KNOW WHAT to do with myself once I'd left. I couldn't stop thinking about Jerry Lee, so I just went back to the hospital. When I saw him he was awake and seemed better and we just sat for a long time not saying anything, just watching the TV. Then finally I couldn't stand it any longer and asked him about the car. He coughed and took a drink of water and looked around to make sure all the other patients were asleep.

'After you left,' he whispered to me, 'I got in the front seat and decided I should go alone. I felt horrible about getting you involved. I'm real sorry I even came by that night, I am. I could get you in trouble, and I never want to do that. That's the last thing I want to do. So I just threw your stuff out and started driving. But I was tired and the weather was bad, and after a while I started seeing things. I hadn't slept much. I didn't know where I was going. I was just driving on 95, north, and then I saw the kid standing in the middle of the road. He was bloody and crying. I tried to stop but I was going too fast. I hit the brakes and almost went off the road, and when I should have hit him, he disappeared and everything went back to normal. That's the way it went. But I didn't stop there. I should have, but I didn't. Finally by sunrise I was in the middle of nowhere.

'I didn't know what to do or where to go 'cause I was so tired. It was like every idea I could have had, good or bad, went out the window. Then I came to this town, I forget the name, but it was small. They had a motel and I got a room and then I went and ate breakfast. I sat in the restaurant and ordered pancakes and bacon. I figured I had to eat. I drank some coffee and started to settle down. I started getting a handle on myself. But when I began eating everything started moving. I thought I might pass out. So I paid the check and went back to the room and got in the bathtub and fell asleep. I woke up a couple hours later when the water turned cold. I almost froze to death. Then I got out and dressed, got back into the car, filled the tank, and bought two five-gallon gas cans and filled them, got some beer, and decided to keep driving. The snow had cleared up, and somebody had plowed. I left the chains on and began taking off-roads, and finally, by dusk, I was lost. The road I was on had snow on it with no other tracks that I could see. There were woods surrounding me in every direction. So I parked the car and went walking around. About a half-mile into them I sat down and drank a few beers. I made sure no one was out there, no cabin or mountain man tooling around. Then I went back to the car, got my sleeping bag and everything I could think of, and stacked as much wood as I could find in the front and back seat. I even put some in the trunk. Then I took the license plates off and tried to scrape off the numbers on the door. It was almost dark by then, by the time I poured gasoline all over the inside and all over the outside and the engine. I started the car and threw a match inside and started running. It burned and burned and I ran until I had to walk and then I just kept walking and eventually made it to a main road and hitchhiked back here. I didn't ever hear it explode like you'd think.

'And I guess it wasn't until the third day of me not being able to sleep that I thought of shooting myself. It seemed like the only good idea I'd had since I hit that kid. I mean, I ain't nobody, I got nothing, and I killed some kid who probably had a big family and a ton of people that liked him and would have helped him out. I ruined all their lives. They're always gonna be in hell. His family always will be, don't you think?'

'I don't know,' I said.

'Well, I know,' Jerry Lee said. 'That's one thing I do know. So don't lie to me and say any different.'

12

OUR MOTHER DIED in a hospital when I was fourteen and my brother was sixteen. I've had a hard time with hospitals ever since. Even when I'm hurting, with a fever or bleeding from a cut, or even when my stomach acts up . . . I won't go. Not unless I'm forced to. They make me that worried. When Polly Flynn drove me to Saint Mary's to see my brother, that was the first time in years that I'd set foot in one.

My mother was a good lady, and I'm not just saying that like you think I would. She rented us a house off Wells Avenue. We had a yard and a porch. She worked as a secretary in the office of an electrical supply company for fifteen years and never complained and was always pretty nice to us, even when she got sick. And her being sick went on for two years. Jerry Lee dropped out of school and got a full-time job with a concrete company and I got a job washing cars on a used lot after school.

By the end all my mother could do was lay on the couch and watch TV or read magazines. She would hardly even eat. But one evening, not long before she died, both Jerry Lee and I came home from being at the river. When we walked in the door we could smell a cake baking in the oven. The kitchen table had a white and red checkered cloth on it and three places were set. My mother stood in the kitchen wearing a dress. She'd made her face up and was wearing a scarf around her head.

'Hello, boys,' she said when she saw us. But even the make-up couldn't hide how pale she was, and her skin hung from her face loose like an old woman. 'Put some clothes on and then come out and sit with me. I bought some steaks, and the grill's lit, but I have to say I'm running out of energy.'

Jerry Lee and I went into our room and changed, then went out to the backyard where she was laying on a lawn chair in the fading evening sun.

'How was swimming?'

'There was no one at our spot, and the water didn't seem that cold.'

'It didn't feel cold at all,' I added.

'Good,' she replied. She wore sunglasses but I could see that her eyes were closed.

'You know,' she said, 'I bought a six-pack of Coke for Jerry Lee and a six-pack of ginger ale for you, Frank.'

Jerry Lee got up and went inside. He reappeared moments later with a Coke, a ginger ale, and a bag of chips.

'You even bought chips,' Jerry Lee said and smiled.

'We're having a party tonight,' she said.

'What's the occasion?' I asked.

'That we're all sitting here. That I have my two boys, that it's sunny out, that you two went swimming. That we have steaks.'

'I'll cook the steaks,' Jerry Lee said.

'Hold on, though,' my mother said. 'Not quite yet. I want to talk to you two for a bit.' She sat up and took off her glasses. 'Now, I don't know what's going to happen, but we have to talk about the options. If something should happen to me, which it might, the only other family I have is in Montana, and I left Montana because of them. Because a lot of things happened there. So I'm not gonna send you there even if I could. I don't know what to do, really, that's the problem. If I can hang on, then soon you'll both be old enough to live on your own. But if not, I think it would be best for you two to stay together, don't you think?'

We both didn't say anything.

'I don't know your dad's family,' she continued. 'I've never even met them. And your dad, we've never really talked about him, but tonight and from now on I'll try. His being in Carson City, in prison, was his fault, and he knew it, and he went in knowing it. But he wasn't mean. He just gambled too much and he stole from his work because of that, and then he got caught. That's not the worst thing anyone has ever done in this world. Believe me it's not. When I knew him, when I fell in love with him, he was a good man. And I did love him, and I'll always love him because he gave me you two. You'd both probably like him, a lot of people did. The thing is, when he got out, he just couldn't adjust back to us. So he left. I don't know where he is now. The last time I heard he was in Laughlin having a hard go of it. That was about seven years ago, maybe a little longer.'

'I don't want to talk about this,' Jerry Lee said and threw his

Coke can out into the yard. He wiped the tears from his face.

'It's not worth it to be mad,' she said in her best calm voice. 'I understand you feeling that way, but it's too much work to be angry. Believe me I know. I've been so angry about this happening, but it doesn't work, it doesn't help. So try not to be, okay?

'Look, I have my retirement plan from work and I'm planning to take it out and set it in a bank account with your names on it. That alone could pay the rent on this place for a couple of years if everything comes through the way it's supposed to. That way you boys will at least have a decent place to stay until Frank's eighteen. The only problem is finding you a legal guardian who will be in charge of you at least in the eyes of the state. I'm working on that. I don't want you two to go into foster care.

'Now if I do die, which I don't plan on, but if I do, there's an old wooden box in my closet, behind all my sweaters, it's an old cigar box, and inside is $500 and my will. The will gives you instructions on what to do with my body, how and where to pay rent. It has title to the car, that sorta thing.'

'You ain't gonna die,' I said to her.

'No, I don't think I will, Frank,' she said. 'I'm trying hard, I really am. But who knows? No one really knows.'

We all sat for a while, none of us talking.

'Okay,' my mother finally said and smiled, 'the last thing is, no matter what, I want you to stay in school. Jerry Lee, you're a wonderful artist and you should keep trying hard at that, and Frank, you're a good student and you play baseball, and sports are good. Do you promise me you'll stay in school?'

We told her we would.

'Good, then that's enough of that. Enough heavy talk for

56

tonight. All right, Jerry Lee, put on the steaks. Frank, when the timer goes off check the cake and if it's done take it out. Check it with a toothpick. If it's done let it cool, then put on the frosting I have sitting on the counter. I made potato salad too, and there's some beans on the stove.'

Jerry Lee and I both got up and did as she said while she stayed sat out in the yard, enjoying the last of the day's sun. I put the radio on low to a country station we all used to listen to and watched Jerry Lee at the barbecue. When the steaks were done we put them on plates with the potato salad and beans, but when we called for her she was asleep on the lawn chair. I put a blanket over her. Jerry Lee and I ate our dinner in silence sitting on the back porch. The sun had lowered by then and you could just make out some stars beginning to appear.

Six months later she passed away. I stuck to my word and was still in school and doing all right at it. Jerry Lee, he'd already quit going. It was spring and I was playing in a baseball game at the high school I went to, on a Saturday. I had been moved up to varsity shortly before. I played second base and the game was in the fifth inning, we were winning by four. I remember a kid was trying to steal second, the catcher threw me the ball and I tagged him out. The kid had slid into me, though, his cleats went into my leg.

'You son of a bitch,' I said.

'Fuck you,' the kid said back.

The umpire called him out, but the kid kept looking back at me as he ran off the field.

After the game I found him standing alone behind the bleachers.

'What do you want?' he said as tough as he could.

I ran at him and began hitting him. I wouldn't stop. I can't remember how long we fought, but in the end he was just laying on the ground and my brother pulled me off him and we left. There was blood on my hands. There was blood all over the kid's face. I didn't stop, when I was on him I mean, I didn't stop hitting him even after he stopped hitting me.

'What the hell did you do that for?' Jerry Lee asked when we had slowed to a walk a half a mile or so away.

'The guy was a real asshole.'

'What did he do?'

'It doesn't matter,' I said.

'You're going crazy,' Jerry Lee said. 'You could have killed him.'

'I ain't going crazy.'

'You can't do shit like that. If you get in trouble, then what do we do? If they call home, then what?'

'I don't know,' I said.

'That was stupid, really fucking stupid.'

'Fuck you,' I said to him.

'You're a stupid bastard,' my brother said and then I swung at him. I hit him in the head, near his left eye and we began fighting. Even though he was older, I got him to the ground and hit him in the face over and over. I broke his nose that day and made both his eyes black. I left him in the yard of some row house, crying and unable to move.

I never went back to school after that day. I quit it all. Even the friends I had I wouldn't see. I wouldn't answer the phone either, and even if I did I just told whoever called that I moved to a different state.

58

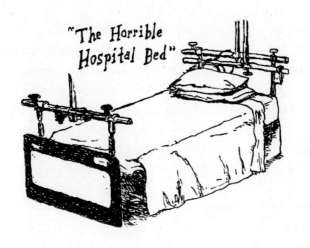

"The Horrible Hospital Bed"

13

THAT NEXT DAY I walked over to Larry's Hideaway Lounge. It's a place behind a grocery store on West Avenue. There's a neon sign that says 'Larry's' and a door. There aren't any windows, no parking places. Inside's a TV, a jukebox, a couple couches, and the bar itself. There are fishing nets on the walls, model boats hanging from the ceiling by fishing line, paintings of the ocean and ships, and a couple dirty fish tanks with half-dead goldfish trying to swim around. It feels like you're in a boat, or maybe in a port in the Philippines, or Thailand, or Japan.

My friend Tommy Locowane, Jerry Lee and I would go there and watch war movies that the owner would play from seven to nine each evening. Not the new ones with blood and guts spurting everywhere, dead babies and flying arms, but the old ones. The ones in the forties and fifties where the guys would be glad to get their legs blown off for their captain and for their country.

So I went in there and I was drinking beer and watching TV when Al Casey came in. He's a guy I met when I was older, in the bars. He's pale and stocky with brown hair; he looks like a boxer, with his nose bent and his face scarred. He was kicked out of college for cheating, and now moved from job to job every couple months. Each time I saw him he looked worse, had gained more weight, bathed less, and dressed more like a bum.

He sat on the stool next to me at the bar and ordered a vodka cranberry.

'Guess where I been?'

'I don't know, where you been?' I said.

'I been in the loony bin, the state mental ward off Glendale,' he said, grinning, and hit the bar with his fist.

'What the hell were you doing in there?'

'I stumbled upon a bottle of liquid acid, and I couldn't stop taking it. Ended up walking down Virginia Street, right down the center of town. All I was wearing was my underwear and my flip-flops.'

'When was this?'

'A month ago.'

'You must've froze your ass off,' I said.

'I didn't feel a thing,' he said and laughed. 'But I woke up in a mess. Luckily I'm still half sane. They say they try to get you straight, but they make you crazier than hell. I ain't ever going there again.'

'I hate hospitals,' I said and finished my beer. I ordered another with a shot of Jim Beam.

'I used to like them okay. At least they're better than working, but Christ, out there, that's no way to live. They had me on all kinds of shit. At least in a real hospital the women look halfway okay, the ones out there, they're ugly as a dead mule.'

'What you doing for work?'

'Just working for my dad. Nothing much. You?'

'I haven't shown up at my job in a week.'

'They'll take you back, won't they?'

'I don't know,' I said as the bartender set down my drinks.

'I moved,' Al said.

'Where to?' I asked.

'My aunt, she's got this garage she lets me live in it. Feels sorry for me. Ain't much, but it's got a wood stove and a toilet. Ain't heard of many garages like that, but that's what it's got.'

'Sounds all right,' I said and drank my shot. I drank half my beer and stood up. 'Well, I'm heading home.'

'Well,' Al said, 'don't get thrown in the mental hospital. It's worse than you'd think.'

'I won't,' I said and walked outside into the night, heading for Saint Mary's.

When I got there I took the elevator up to Jerry Lee's room. He was asleep, but the TV was on. I pulled a chair next to him and took the remote and began going through the channels.

'Hey there,' he said.

I looked over at him and he yawned and tried to wake.

'They say anything about your leg?'

'They ain't sure. Just depends if they can stop some infection I guess I got. At least I shot myself in the leg that was already bad.'

'Yeah,' I said.

'You're drunk, hunh?'

'Yeah,' I said and smiled.

'I wish I was. It's so boring in here. Their TV sucks too. They got cable, but not much else. Where did you go?'

'The Hideaway.'

'You heard anything about the kid?'

'No,' I said. 'But I ain't looked in the paper or anything. I just been moping around.'

'Me too,' he said. 'I'm tired as shit. I'm sorry if I fall back asleep.'

'I don't mind. I'm just gonna sit here for a while.'

'I'm glad you're here,' he said and closed his eyes and drifted off.

I sat there and watched TV for an hour or so, then I found a pen and a pad of paper in the drawer next to him and wrote him a story hoping it would help pass the time and give him a break from the TV.

Jerry Lee,

Well . . . you've probably been wondering where I been? Well . . . I don't know why I did it, but I stole almost twenty grand from my dad, Dick Senior, on his credit card. His emergency card. His card for the pawn shop. We have the same name. Dick Van Buren is my dad, and I'm Dickie Van Buren. I was gone for over two months. I guess he didn't check the card until after I was done, until his accountant brought it to his attention.

I rented a car and drove to Carson City, and I stayed at the old Ormsby House. It's a nice place. I got a room with a king-size bed, a bed the size of a car. I spent three days on it ordering in from room service and watching TV. Then I went down to a department store and bought a few suits. One black, one brown, one green. I'd never worn a suit in my life, but I wanted to look different, you know? I got two pairs of J.C. Penney imitation wing tips, a gray overcoat, a few packs of underwear, and a couple packs of socks.

Then I drove over to the Cotton Tail Ranch. I met a girl named Deana and over the course of a week I spent $4,000 on her. She had some huge tits. They were amazing. They were fake, but it was a real pro job, you could tell. I can't begin to explain what got into me, really, it's the god's honest truth I can't. Maybe it was just that first night she and me sat in the hot tub. I spent a couple hours in there with her, nothing much, just the normal. Smoked a little weed, talked about dancing. But she was good. Let me just make that clear. She was damn good. Then when I was done I paid her and left. No big deal, right?

But the thing is, I couldn't get her out of my mind. The next day I picked her again and had her dress in black leather. I paid her to get under the covers with me and bite me on the chest while I spanked her ass. Jesus, I don't know why.

The day after I talked to her and her madam, and for $1,000 up front I got to take her out of the brothel. I wanted to play a game of tennis with her. I bought her a racket and a tennis outfit. I thought I'd kick her ass, but she beat me three games straight. Six-love, six-three, six-four. Who would have thought?

We changed in the hotel room, ate lunch together, then went back to the brothel where I picked her and another girl named Lara. We all sat in the hot tub, and let me tell you it got crazy. Everybody on everybody. A real free for all.

I saw her every day that week. On the last day I finally said why the fuck not, and I read her one of my stories. Did I ever tell you I wrote stories?

63

Well, the one I read was called 'Lyndon Johnson and his Encounters with Aliens from Space while Driving to Reno'. I read it to her while she sat on her knees and gave me a blow job. The story's not about ex-President Lyndon Johnson, but another Lyndon Johnson who owned an auto body shop in Las Vegas. This Lyndon Johnson was abducted by creatures from space, and while there was probed and dissected. Then the aliens dropped him back to earth as a child. They had made Lyndon ten years old, bald, and so traumatized by the whole ordeal that he never spoke again. It's not a bad story, but not one of my best either.

Anyway, after I was done, she said I should go down to LA. The story, she told me, was that good. She thought it would make a great movie. She even told me the last hummer was on the house. She was that impressed. She gave me a hug. She kissed me right on the lips for Christsakes. So I put on my clothes, put my story of Lyndon Johnson in my coat pocket, slipped her a hundred, and walked out. I decided right then I was going to drive all the way to Los Angeles, California. Was I crazy? I don't know. Maybe, but she may have had a point, who knows? I checked out of the hotel and left that day. That first night I got a motel in Bishop, California. The next morning I gave a ride to this guy who was hitchhiking to Long Beach. He and I got high, so I didn't give a shit about anything. I took out one of my stories, and had the man read it. I told him if he wanted to ride with me that was his payment. It was one called 'In the Ruby Mountains, Ten below Zero, Snow Storm, Lost and Left for Dead by Aliens. The Amazing Story of Donny Dibble.'

The thing is, the guy had a great speaking voice. It was like he was a radio man on the lam. After he had finished it, hell, I was even impressed that I wrote it. The hitchhiker said he couldn't believe I could write such a tremendous work of art. He wouldn't stop talking about it. The whole way down, the guy went on about it.

I dropped him off on the side of the road somewhere in LA and then went to a motel called the Ocean View on Sunset Boulevard. I rented a room for a week and became a shut-in. A man with a mission. I wrote four stories. I don't know what got into me. Inspiration is a miracle, a pinnacle of light at times. The first one was 'Alone in the Tundra of North Canada with a Toothbrush and a Spool of Wire: A Story of Survival'. The second, 'The Radiation Man and his Search for his Lost and Forgotten Radiation Planet'. Then while taking a bath I wrote 'Help = Death on Mars'.

The final story, and maybe my only masterpiece, I wrote after going to a strip club on Hollywood Blvd. It was a nasty, nasty place, but I saw this little Asian chick named Candy and I wrote my first and only love story, 'Hey, Candy, It's Me, Romeo!'.

Then the craziest thing happened. I was driving around Hollywood when I saw an old woman get run over by a city bus. She was in the middle of the street trying to chase down this white poodle who'd run into the traffic. I pulled over to the side of the street. Then the bus nailed her. I ran over to see what had happened. The bus driver was standing over her. She was dead, you could tell. The bus driver broke down. How could this happen? the guy screamed in tears of rage and sorrow. How could something like this have happened? How? How? How? My life is ruined all over a dog who got loose!?

When the police came, I gave them a statement and they took pictures and wrote things down. Then the ambulance came and took the old lady away. I felt bad for the bus driver. He was a real mess. They asked about the dog, but no one knew where it was. The officers thanked me for sticking around. No problem, I said. But I knew then I was going to get the hell out of LA. Adios amigo! So I trotted back to my car. But Jesus Christ if I didn't see the dog on the way. Hiding in the bushes on the side of the road.

I waited until the police officers were looking the other way, and then I ran over to it. I took off my coat, threw it over the poodle's head, grabbed it, and sprinted to my car. I opened the trunk and threw it in. I looked in the rear-view mirror as I drove off, but no one noticed anything. I drove side streets for hours looking for the cops or an undercover tail, but I had lost them, given them the slip, as they say. So I eased up, turned on the radio, and went to a grocery store and bought a gallon of bottled water, a five-pound bag of dog food, and a plastic bone and snuck the dog into my motel room.

I decided to move to Alaska that night. The last frontier. The last place in America for freedom, for individuality, for honor, for peace. It's also a great place to raise a dog. I dropped off the rental car, took a cab to a used car lot, and picked up a 1975 Ford Bronco for $2,000. On the way out of town I picked up a sleeping bag, winter clothes, a camping stove, freeze-dried food, an ax, and a fishing pole.

Ten days later I was sitting in a bar in Juneau, Alaska. Some of the weirdest people I'd ever seen in my life live up there. I spent the first week in a motel watching TV and reading Jack London. Got through most of his whole collection. I wanted to study, I really did, but after reading White Fang I knew that the wilderness was no place to live. Have you read that fucking book? You'd have to be nuts to live like that. Out in a cabin with no TV and no

66

heat. And then it dawned on me, I got a fucking poodle, not a husky. I'd need a fucking husky, but then I liked the poodle. I didn't know what to do.

So I drove the truck down to Portland, Oregon, got a motel room, and spent a couple weeks watching cable TV and playing with the dog. But then I started getting homesick, real homesick. I don't know why I did, but I did. We all know this town is a shit-hole. But it's my shithole. Then I freaked out and bought a solid gold wristwatch with diamonds on it for my dad. It cost a fucking fortune. Or cost him. Ha! Ha! Ha! Shit, anyway, I had it engraved, 'To the best dad I know, love Dickie Jr.' I drove back to Reno the same day they finished the watch. Then I was in Grants Pass at a rest stop, and I let the dog out to take a leak. Problem was, when I was ready to go I just got back in the car and drove off. I forgot about the dog. I was almost in Reno by the time I remembered, but by then I was too tired to go back.

Anyway, I gave my dad the watch and he didn't know what to think. Then a couple days later he found out about the card, and the son of a bitch committed me to a private mental hospital for evaluation. Can you believe that? But I didn't give a shit. Why should I? It's better than working. At least that's what I thought at the time.

The first guy I met in there said he's Liberace's son. I said Jesus, Liberace didn't have a kid. So we got in a fight, it was touch and go for a while then I kicked the shit out of him and ended up in the state mental ward. It took me three months to get out of there, but it wasn't as bad as you'd think.

Signed your pal,
Dickie Junior

I don't know what time it was when I was done, but the nurse finally kicked me out, so I set the story on Jerry Lee's chest and made my way home.

14

I GOT UP THAT NEXT MORNING, took a shower, shaved, put on some clothes and walked to my old job at the restaurant supply and repair company. The day was sunny, cold out, but there was no breeze and the walking warmed me up. The place I worked was on Virginia Street. I was a local driver, sometimes I'd go on longer trips with another guy to Fallon or to Lake Tahoe, but mostly it was just around town picking up and delivering fryers and ovens, doing repairs and installations, things like that.

I didn't want to go in there since I hadn't called or told them why I hadn't shown up for over a week, and when I got there I could see that the truck I used was gone, so figured they'd found someone new. I went in there anyway, though, and the main boss said a few things to me, then took me into his office and sat me down in one of his leather chairs. He was an all right guy, but he was mad and he wouldn't stop talking about how mad he was.

Then he started up on his business, his family, honor, pride, and sales. I didn't say anything, and when he was done I just thanked him for the job. I went to the accounting lady, got my last paycheck, and left.

After I cashed it, I walked over to the Gun Rack where my friend Tommy Locowane worked for his Uncle Gary. The place was an old brick building on Wells Street. It had been around for years, ever since I could remember. On the left was a pet store, and on the right a carpet store. The pet store was an old place too, a place where my mom would buy fish for a tank we had when I was a kid.

That morning Tommy was alone sitting at the counter eating breakfast.

'Want an Egg McMuffin?' he asked when he saw me. A radio was playing in the background, and he was reading the newspaper.

'All right,' I said and leaned against the counter. He handed me one then got up and went into the back room and came out with a cup of coffee in an old Harrah's coffee mug.

'Sugar only?'

'Yeah,' I said, took the cup from him, and set it on the counter.

I'd known Tommy from when I was a kid, from high school. We'd been friends since the day we met. His mom had left them back then, and him and his dad fought all the time after that.

His dad would hit him, give him a black eye, bruise his ribs, things like that. So he began to stay with Jerry Lee and me. He did that on and off until he was seventeen, when he finally moved out of his dad's house for good and in with his Uncle Gary, his mom's brother.

Tommy's half Scottish, half Paiute Indian. His build is average, but he's gaining weight all in his stomach and in his face. He eats worse than me or even Jerry Lee. Cans of Dinty Moore Stew and candy bars, fast food, and twelve-packs of soda. He's always drinking soda, always has one open. He's not good looking either, girls don't like him.

'Sorry to hear about your brother,' he said and shook his head. 'I went by yesterday and sat with him.'

'I'm going by this afternoon,' I said.

'Why do you think he did it?'

'I'm not sure,' I said.

'Must've hurt,' Tommy said.

'Yeah,' I said.

'The last time he was in the hospital was for his leg too. It was almost a month he was in then, wasn't it?'

I nodded.

'You know, seeing him in there like that, I couldn't help but think about that night we all hopped that train. That was one of the worst nights I've ever had.'

'I've been thinking about that as well,' I said.

'It's hard not to,' Tommy said.

The phone rang then and he answered it. It was his uncle, and as they spoke my mind wandered back to that night by the railroad tracks.

Jerry Lee, Tommy, and I were at our old house, the one my mom left for us. We were drinking in the kitchen. I was fifteen. We decided we'd catch a freight train to San Francisco. I don't know why exactly, just one of those things we used to sit around and think about. An adventure. We all dressed in our warmest clothes, and I had a pack and filled it with beer, some beef jerky, and a couple blankets. We walked down Fourth Street and then cut over to the tracks and sat in the darkness, drank beers and waited.

But hours passed and nothing happened, no train at all. I remember Jerry Lee had fallen asleep against a concrete piling, and Tommy and I were still drinking when a train finally came heading west. I can't remember what time it was, but it was late, probably near dawn. I shook Jerry Lee awake as the train arrived, and we all got up and stood ready to catch it as it slowed through town sounding its horn in the quiet darkness. There were a few lumber cars and on them there were pockets where you could hide, so we decided we'd try for one of them. We picked a car and ran alongside chasing the metal ladder at the end of it. Tommy got on first, then me, but by this time the train had picked up speed again, and Jerry Lee, who was last, fell as he tried to get on. His leg, just below his knee, went under the train.

We both jumped off, not real sure of what was going on. He wasn't even screaming, and all we knew for sure was that he didn't make it. The train was moving pretty quickly by then and when I jumped off I fell and landed wrong on my arm. When I stood up I could see something pushing out my coat. I slowly took my parka off and you could see the bone pressing out against my flannel shirt. Tommy came running to me saying that Jerry Lee had gotten his leg cut off.

We went over and Tommy took off his belt and used it as a tourniquet, and then he wrapped a blanket around the stump and ran for help.

By the time the ambulance came only ten minutes had gone by. It was that fast, or at least it seemed like it. I remember while we waited I sat next to Jerry Lee. He was in shock and wasn't saying anything, just sorta staring at the sky. I wasn't sure what to do, I just held his hand and looked at him and told him he would be okay.

They found his leg and we brought it with us in the ambulance. They did things to him, put oxygen on him, started an IV, put some sorta thing over where his leg was. The leg itself they put in a bag. I couldn't see it, though, I wasn't sure where they kept it. I just sat there while the ambulance drove us the short distance to the hospital, and it wasn't until they had brought him in, and he had disappeared to the emergency room, that I finally showed someone my arm.

It took a long time until they came to get me. Finally they took me to a room and numbed my arm and set the bone, sewed it up and put on a cast.

Jerry Lee was in the hospital for four weeks. We didn't have any insurance. Our mother had been gone only six months, and the money she had left, we used on the hospital bill. It was a terrible time: Jerry Lee lost his leg, and we were in constant fear that they'd send us off to a foster home. My mom's father from Montana was called and eventually came down to Reno. He met with the Children Services, as he was supposed to be our legal guardian. He stayed in town almost three weeks. He seemed like an okay guy, but both Jerry Lee and I weren't sure about him and were nervous about living with him in Montana. But he and I moved us out of our old place and got rid of all our things, like the beds and the furniture, the dishes and the TV. We kept only what was small and a necessary. My grandfather got a room at the Virginian and I moved in there with him.

When Jerry Lee was finally getting better my grandfather decided that he couldn't have us up in Montana after all, that he didn't have enough room, that he was too old, that he didn't have enough money. He was a retired mill worker. His back was wrecked and he lived on social security. I remember he stood in the hospital room and gave us $200 and his phone number, saying that he'd try to get us up there as soon as he could, if he could at all. He left the day that Jerry Lee was released.

When the time came we had a wheelchair and I pushed him out of the hospital down Fourth Street in the early sunlight. We didn't know where to go, and finally just got a room at the Rancho Motel. I paid in advance for two weeks, and that left us with less than thirty dollars between us.

I remember then making two trips. The first was to get our things I'd left with the Locowanes, and the second was to the store, where I bought two loaves of bread, a jar of peanut butter, a glass jar of jam, and a TV guide. When I got back Jerry Lee was laying on the bed watching the television. He said while I was gone he'd heard people yelling in the room next to us and had gotten scared, and the only thing that made sense to him was ordering a pizza. A large with pepperoni, mushrooms, and olives. When the pizza man came, I gave him the money, and tipped him with our second to last dollar.

'Well, Frank,' Tommy's uncle said, bringing me back to where I was. 'Frank, I wondered if you'd like to make a few bucks today?'

I nodded and told him of course I did.

It was an errand, he said, to pick up five guns from a broker in Carson City. He gave me the keys to his car and directions, and so I filled up my coffee and headed out the door.

74

15

THE JOB I HAD when my mother passed away had been washing cars under the table at Hurley's Used Auto Hamlet. This was before the accident, before we needed more money. I did it after school, and on Saturdays and Sundays. My bosses were the old man, Earl Hurley, and his grandson Barry, a guy who always wore light blue suits and drank Budweiser. He was married to a real great looking girl named Helen, who wore sunglasses all the time. You couldn't help but stare at her. I remember I'd bring Jerry Lee by sometimes when I knew she'd be there just so he could see her. She and Barry were always together; they were in love with each other and most evenings when I was there she'd stop by on her way home from work and pick up a different car.

She drove a different one every day of the week, or at least every day she felt like it, I guess. On Saturdays she would bring us food. Sometimes Chinese, or Mexican, or sub sandwiches. A couple times in the summer she'd set up the grill there at the lot, and we'd have a barbecue. She'd wear an apron and her hair would be pulled back and she always wore shorts and a tight T-shirt.

But it was Earl, the old man and head boss, who I really got to know. He was the one that I always went to talk to. He's the one that's probably the greatest man I know.

Right after my mother died, maybe a couple weeks later, I was washing this car, it was a Saturday, middle of the day. I even remember the car, an American Motors Company 1985 Eagle. A copper/gold four door. I had rinsed it down and was beginning to wash it when I stopped, and just stood there, frozen almost, and began crying. I was doing that quite a bit back then. It was hard to explain, but sometimes, out of nowhere, I'd just stop and daze off and I'd cry or I'd start hyperventilating and I wouldn't be able to stop.

I guess that time, the time I'm talking about, Earl had been watching me 'cause he came out of the office and walked over to me.

'It's all right, son,' he said in a soft voice as he neared me. He was smoking a cigarette. He had sunglasses on, the kind that lighten in darkness and darken in light, and he wore a brown suit with white dress shoes.

'You all right?'

'What?' I barely got out.

'I said, are you all right?' He was smiling. 'You in there?'

I just looked at him. I was unable to speak. The tears were still running down my face.

'First thing is, drop the sponge and fuck this car,' he said. 'Probably no use even washing it. We'll probably never sell this son of a bitch anyway. AMCs are worthless. For a time they were all right, but the later models, Jesus, they just went to hell. You hungry? It's about that time, let's go get a bite to eat.'

I dropped the sponge I had in a bucket. I wiped the tears from my eyes with my shirt. Barry was sitting in the front office watching TV when Earl told him we were going for some food.

'Get me something too,' Barry said.

'What do you want?' Earl said.

'I don't know, where you guys going?'

'We're gonna go eat the puss out of a dead hog's ass,' Earl said in his gruff voice and lit another cigarette.

'Get me mine without ketchup,' Barry said and laughed.

'Will do' was all old man Hurley said as we left.

He drove us in a 1994 Cadillac two-door Seville to a place called the Halfway Club on Fourth Street. An Italian place run by an old lady, a woman who'd run it for years and years. Maybe forty years. I can't remember exactly if it's that long, but it's close.

Earl ordered me a Coke and himself a Long Island Ice Tea.

'I'm sorry as hell about your mother,' he said while we were looking at the menu. He was smoking a cigarette, and you could almost see the lenses on his glasses change in the dimly lit room. 'When I lost my wife, I about lost my fucking mind, and, shit, you're only, what, sixteen?'

'I just turned fifteen,' I said.

'I hired you when you were fourteen?'

'Yeah,' I said.

He laughed and shook his head.

'Did I ask you your age?'

77

'No,' I said.

'Did you tell me you were sixteen?'

'No,' I said. 'I was too nervous to mention age at all.'

'What the hell was I thinking?' he said and shook his head again. 'Anyway, that's beside the point. How's your living situation, is it okay? I want you to be honest, son.'

'My brother and me are living at our old house.'

'You rent or own?'

'Rent,' I said.

'That's a setback. Your brother, he's what, eighteen?'

'Seventeen,' I said.

'You got no other family?'

'Not really, I don't think so. We had a grandfather but he turned out to be a real son of a bitch,' I said.

'You got any money?'

'My mom's retirement fund. We have that and we both work. It's enough, I think.'

'What you guys eat?'

'Frozen dinners, we eat at Jim Boys a lot. Burger King, places like that.'

'You got to eat better than that. At least hit the buffets. Get a salad, some fruit and vegetables once in a while. Get some vitamins.' He stopped, took a drink, then went into his billfold and took from it a twenty-dollar bill. 'This here's for a big bottle of vitamins. Get some sorta multi, make your brother take them too. If I find you pissed the twenty away on anything else, I'll castrate you. Understand?'

'Understand,' I said and took the money. I folded it and put it in my pants pocket.

78

'What do you two do at night?'

'Watch TV mostly.'

'What kind?'

'Sitcoms, I guess. Whatever's on.'

'You got to quit that,' he said. 'TV's for fucking morons.'

'I know,' I said.

'I'm serious.'

'I'll try to lay off some.'

'Good,' Earl said. 'How's school? You still playing baseball?'

'Yeah, I'm playing all right. I'm starting on second. They moved me up to varsity. Jerry Lee, my brother, just dropped out. Sometimes I think I might too. Doesn't seem like there's much there except sports, and I really don't like them that much anymore.'

'Don't drop out,' Earl said and took a long drink off the Long Island, nearly finishing it. 'You won't miss anything if you don't quit. All you'll do is wash more cars or get some other stupid fucking job. You'll never see any girls around, none your age, and they won't touch you 'cause you're not in school and you have no money. Girls love baseball players. You keep playing and you'll be set. What's your brother do?'

'Works for Connelly Concrete.'

'See what I mean. That's gotta be a horrible fucking job.'

'I know,' I said.

'His back will be gone by the time he's forty.'

I nodded my head.

'It's convict labor, son. You two ain't convicts, so don't start acting like it,' he said and took the napkin off the table and wiped his brow. 'Your brother still drawing?'

79

'That's all he does. Sketches things, makes comics, things like that.'

'I liked that naked girl he drew standing in front of the lot. I had it framed and keep it at the house. How'd he get into that?'

'I don't know exactly. He started it more when our mom got sick. He'd just sit in front of the TV and draw. I think he's taken some classes.'

'Tell him he'll get laid a lot more if he stays in school and hangs out with art girls. God knows there's a lot of them beating around. See if that changes his mind at all.'

'I will.'

'What were you thinking out there? I mean, when you were just standing there. I think I clocked you at ten minutes, maybe fifteen. I didn't see you move once. Just standing there with the hose.'

'I just started thinking about stuff. I'm not sure why it happens. I don't know, guess I get scared, and sometimes I sorta black out because of it.'

'I'd be scared too. If I were you I'd be shitting in my pants. It's hard being alone.'

'I'll be all right.'

'I hope so. There's a good chance you might be,' he said and looked for the old lady who ran the place. When she came around he ordered another drink and another Coke for me.

'Seems like you're a pretty tough kid. Look, here's a piece of advice. I don't know if it's any good or not for you, you're the only one who'll know if it is. What you got to do is think about the life you want, think about it in your head. Make it a place where you want to be: a ranch, a beach house, a penthouse on the top of a skyscraper. It doesn't matter what it is, but a place that you can hide out in. When things get rough, go there. And if you find a place and it quits working, just change it. Change it depending on the situation, depending on your mood. Look at it this way, it'll be like your good luck charm. Make up a place that's good, that gives you strength, that no one can take away. Then when everybody's on your ass, or you can't stop thinking about your mom, you can go there.'

'Okay,' I said.

'Does that make sense?'

'I think so,' I said. 'Could it help my brother Jerry Lee?'

'I don't know. Tell him to try it. Or tell him about yours. I used to tell Barry stories all the time when his life was rough. Some of them were true, others I just made up, but they seemed to help him out. Gave him a place to escape to, gave him hope. Hope is the key. You can make shit up, there's no law against that. Make up some place you and your brother can go if you want. It might not work, but it might. Ain't too hard to try.'

'Do you have a place you go?'

'Sure,' he said, 'I go to it a couple times a day. Being an old man, I can't sleep worth a shit anymore, sometimes late at night I'll just lay there, and wonder what the fuck I'm going to do. I'm sleeping with nothing but a couple old dogs who steal the covers, I own a half-ass used car lot, and I can't stop drinking. Sure, I got a place.'

'The lot's great,' I said.

'Shit, kid, it's a waste of fucking time,' he said.

'You keep getting more cars,' I said.

'That's not the point. I'm not the point,' he said and smiled. 'You're the point.'

'I'll get a place,' I said.

'Good,' he said. 'I hope it helps. If you need anything, anything at all, just let me know. I'm not bullshitting about that either. Let me or Barry know. Barry's a good one, he's been through the wringer so he might be able to help you out more than me. I'm talking money and advice. If you get in any trouble, shit like that. It's easy to get in trouble when you first get out on your own. Everyone does. You probably will, so just let me know. And try to stay in school. I'm serious. Life can fuck you hard. You got to be smart about the decisions you make. School's easy, there's girls, you can get free lunch there, you can probably get breakfast too, it's more or less peaceful. Better than working for Connelly Concrete.'

'I'll try,' I said.

'Good,' he said and smiled. 'Now let's eat. They got great ravioli and great pizza. The service is slow, the old lady keeps getting older, but she can still cook, and we don't have any place we got to be either. Barry can fend for himself.'

'All right,' I said and smiled at him. 'But we got to remember to get him something to eat.'

'Good memory, son. After this,' he said, 'I'm thinking we'll either go bowling or maybe go down to the Cal Neva and you can watch me gamble.'

That evening as I lay in bed I stared out the window into the black, starless sky. Jerry Lee was moving around in his bed, I could hear him, and I knew he wasn't asleep either. It was past midnight when finally I called to him and told him what Earl Hurley had said that day.

'Makes sense to me,' Jerry Lee announced when I had finished.

'Me too, I guess,' I said.

'I like Earl Hurley.'

'He's a good guy,' I said. 'We ate ravioli and steaks for lunch. He drank four Long Island Iced Teas, and then I spent three hours watching him play roulette at the Cal Neva.'

'What's in those again?' Jerry Lee asked.

'Long Islands?'

'Yeah.'

'I don't know, but they're strong. I took a drink off one of his while he was in the can, and it almost made me puke.'

'I like ravioli,' he said. 'It's probably in my top five favorite meals. Shit, I wished I worked for him and not for the Connelly brothers.'

'It's a pretty good job,' I said.

'Seems like it. Anyway,' Jerry Lee said, 'what's your place gonna be like?'

'I don't know yet,' I said, still unsure of what Earl was really talking about.

'I'm making a place where the Connelly brothers have to work for me. And I'll beat the shit out of them every couple weeks, and I'll get it on with their wives. I'll fuck both their wives at the same time, while they're busting their ass for me, up to their hips in wet concrete. "Hurry up, you lazy son of a bitches," I'll yell. Then I'd bury my head in one of the bosses' wives' tits.'

We both began laughing.

'I don't know where I'm going,' I finally said, 'but you'll be there, and so will Mom.'

'That's a nice thought, Frank,' Jerry Lee said. 'If you come up with any good ones, let me know.'

'I will,' I said.

'Now let's go to bed,' he said, ''cause, unlike you, I got to get up at five a.m. and get yelled at all day by the Connellys.'

'Night,' I said.

'Night,' he said and rolled over. I stared back out the window and tried to be still. In time I heard the slow rhythm of Jerry Lee's breathing and I knew he was asleep. When I woke the next morning at seven he was already gone and his bed was made.

16

WHEN VISITING HOURS ENDED I left the hospital and wandered around. I wasn't tired, but I didn't want to see anyone, and I didn't want to go back to my room and sit there all alone. So I went downtown to the strip. The neon lights glowed in the cold, and I felt better just seeing them. Casinos always make me feel better, and I can't really even explain why. 'Cause when you look at it, really look at it, mostly all they cause is misery.

I walked around for a long time, down Virginia Street then along Second Street and Center Street. I went in and out of Harrahs and the Fitz and the Eldorado and the Cal Neva. When my feet began to get cold I finally went back to my room. A maintenance man had come in and fixed the broken window. They didn't believe me about the bird and said I was going to have to pay for the window and the labor. I said I would, but I knew I couldn't, that I had less than sixty dollars to my name, and it didn't seem like I could get a job with the way I was feeling.

I turned the lights off and undressed as the small box heater glowed in the darkness. I turned my electric blanket on and got into my bed. From there I can stare out at Fourth Street. I can see if any people walk by, or just watch the cars passing in the night.

It was then as I lay there watching the street below that a horrible feeling came down over me. I felt that the room was going to catch fire and that I'd die in flames and smoke. That I might have a heart attack. That I might die before I hit a good stretch in my life. That Jerry Lee would die. The uncertainty of everything. Spinning and spinning round. It went on like that, even when the electric blanket had kicked in. It was all horrible, the thoughts in my mind were, and I can't begin to tell you why they started or why they wouldn't stop. I began getting the shakes, like I was a kid and somebody was yelling at me. I couldn't control it and finally I had to make myself get up, get dressed, and leave the room.

I walked down two flights of stairs and was going to head back downtown when I saw the lights on in the old kitchen and went in there and saw the manager, Claire Martin. She was a friend of my mother's and the only reason I had moved into the Morris.

When I saw her she was standing over the stove cooking breakfast. Ham and eggs, potatoes and toast. Coffee was brewing. She was wearing a faded, light blue bathrobe, and wore a pair of worn-out white slippers. Her gray and black hair was pulled together in a bun. There was a yellow school pencil keeping it tight and together.

'Morning, Frank,' she said quietly when she saw me. 'If you want breakfast I have more than enough.'

'Thank you,' I said and sat down at the table. I wasn't hungry, but the smell was good, and I knew I didn't want to be alone. That I'd probably go crazy if I was.

I watched her while she cooked. The radio was on to the old folks' station and she hummed softly with the music. When the food was ready she dished out two plates and sat down across from me, and we ate together in silence. I didn't think I could eat, but I got down the whole plate. I had two cups of coffee with it and began to feel better.

When we had both finished she picked up the plates and set them in the sink. She lit a cigarette, filled our coffee cups, and sat back down at the table.

'You know, Frank, I've smoked a lot of brands of cigarettes over the years. When I was in high school I smoked Marlboros because that was what my mom and dad smoked. Then of course I switched, went from Winstons to Old Golds, then to Camels. Now it doesn't seem to matter. Now I just smoke generics. I can't even tell the difference. But I do love opening that new pack and taking the first one out knowing I have the rest of the pack waiting. You ever smoke?'

'No,' I said. 'I tried it. Both me and Jerry Lee did, but it didn't work. I used to chew, though.'

'What brand?'

'Copenhagen.'

'Like my own brother. That's a horrible habit.'

'It is,' I said.

'You quit?'

'Yeah.'

'Good for you. What made you do it?'

'I was going out with a girl. She didn't like it.'

Claire laughed and took a drink of coffee.

'What are you doing up so early? I thought you always slept late.'

'It's my anniversary.'

'You're married?'

'I was,' she said and took a drink from her coffee and knocked the ash from her cigarette.

'Where is he?'

'He died.'

'I'm sorry.'

'It was a long time ago.'

'What was he like?'

'He wasn't much of a man, but things with me were different back then. Your mom knew him and knew how I was with him. I could barely make a pot of coffee without thinking that I would ruin it or somehow screw it up. Every job I had was that way. I was always worried. Worried if I cleaned a table right, smiled right to a customer. Then I worked in an office, that's where I met your mom. But I worried about everything. From how I stapled two pieces of paper together to how my voice projected over the phone. My husband was the type who'd get angry at things like that. At the little mistakes I made, little screw-ups that happened during the course of each day.

'Luckily for me, I suppose, he died in a car wreck,' she said and laughed. 'It's horrible to say that, but it's the truth. Even so, I can't drive near our old house without feeling sick, and I can't look at a pack of Lucky Strike cigarettes and not get nervous. They were his brand.'

'I'm sorry,' I said.

'Like I said, it was a long time ago. How's Jerry Lee?'

'I don't want to talk about that either.'

'Let's talk about something nice then,' Claire said.

'All right,' I said.

'All right,' she said and laughed. 'Problem is, I'm not sure what else to talk about. You tell me something, Frank.'

'I could tell you a story that I always tell Jerry Lee when he gets down.'

'Good,' she said. 'I like stories. Let's hear it.'

'Well,' I said, 'you remember Annie James?'

'She was your girlfriend?'

'Yeah.'

'Kind of, but my memory's fading. You had her before you moved in here, correct?'

'Correct,' I said. 'Well, anyway, once she and I double dated with Jerry Lee and a girl named Lorraine. That was his girl. It was a picnic. We were all sitting on the grass at this park eating. Lorraine was talking about her cousin Harvey. This poor kid had to live hard for a while, maybe like you did. His life was different, he was just a kid, and he was a boy, but maybe it will make sense to you.

'See, no one gave him a break. He lived in North Dakota with his mom, Lorraine's aunt. I remember Lorraine talking to Annie about it. She was sitting there pulling out grass with her fingers as she told it. Me and Jerry Lee were sitting there eating cold barbecue chicken that Annie had made the night before. It was good chicken too. Lorraine started by saying, "If you think that's bad, well listen about my cousin, my cousin Harvey. He was a big foot-

89

ball player type. Six five, three hundred pounds. Now that's huge
if you ask me. And he was just in high school. He was the ape of
the family. He was so big, I can't even begin to describe it. Like
the Hulk. But fatter, not as much muscle showing. When he was a
kid, before he had to play football, my Aunt Carol signed poor
Harvey up for boxing. He was in a boxing club. But he wasn't very
good. It was terrible to watch.

"'I once saw him fight when he was maybe thirteen. It's sick,
boxing is, but there we were. My whole family. Eating popcorn
and licorice, drinking sodas. Harvey stood there getting muti-
lated. They try not to let the little guys get so beat up, but he just
stood there and finally fell to the floor. I don't think he got off even
one punch. I don't think he even tried.

"'And it was like that, I guess, at every match. Then by high
school he's huge, a mountain. So he goes out for football. Aunt
Carol's feeding him steaks and meat every day. He's practically
eating whole cows. She's sending us pictures. One picture he's
huge and the next he's even bigger. Really, in six months he'd get
bigger. 'Jesus Christ,' my mom would say to me, 'that kid's a goddamn pig. My sister's raising a goddamn pig!'

"'So they stick him on varsity football 'cause he's so big. He's
the biggest guy on the team. He was only a freshman but still
probably one of the biggest guys in the school. That's how big he
was. But the same thing happens. He just gets beat up. He's not
mean. The coach says he's got the size and strength and speed to
make it to the pros, but that he's just not mean enough. The asshole coach would even make him do these drills trying to beat him
up, get him mad. Everybody figured that if he'd get tough he'd be
a gold mine. A pile of money. My aunt would yell at him. Call him

names, make him work for his meals and his bed. He'd get home from practice and then have to do chores. Once he had to chop this dead tree down. It was an old big tree on their lot, and by the time he got home it was dark and freezing out. He'd have to go out there with a big light and chop it into sections that they could use. Then he had to dig out the stump. He had to do tons of things like that, and then he'd go in and eat, and she'd yell at him. This went on for three years. But by the start of the football season his senior year, everybody had given up. They'd tried everything. There was no way this kid was going to get mean. Isn't that just insane? Wanting to make a person mean. So big Harvey quits football by the second game of his senior year. Everybody by this time knows he's not tough. I hate to say wimp, but that's what everybody called him. He couldn't escape it. Aunt Carol was going out with an ex-Marine type by this time. Harvey was getting it from all sides. It's sad. This is small-town America. The Midwest we're talking about. Everything. So what happens is that Harvey just sits in his room. Goes to school, comes home, and sits in his room. He has the Marine on his ass all the time, and people calling him a wimp at school. Never ending. Over and over. Anyway, what the whole thing came down to is that poor Harvey shaves his head with his electric razor one morning, puts on a dress of Aunt Carol's, and walks down to where she's working. She works at a chain-link fence manufacturing plant with a bunch of hicks, perverts, and ex-Marines. He goes down there. Goes right into where everybody is, goes up to Aunt Carol, and screams, 'Mama, I don't think I can have sex with you no more. I don't think it's right. I don't think it's right at all.' He's dead serious too. From what I know she never touched him. But everybody's there watching, listening. What a mess. Can you imagine that?

'"Anyway, from what I hear, she practically died. She should have. Making him do all those horrible things. Trying to make him mean. So then he just walks out of there. Aunt Carol didn't know what to do. So she runs into the bathroom, and won't come out. She hides out in there. She was in there all day. Finally, they broke the door down. Took an ax to it. They were worried that she might kill herself. But she was just sitting there on the toilet crying. Anyway, what happens is that Harvey disappears. No one sees him after that day. He had the keys to the Marine's car, and he took it and disappeared. He went to California, and started his own life. He sends my mom Christmas cards and postcards now and then. Ended up inventing a bunch of stuff for computers, turned out to be a genius. Now he owns three houses and a ranch in the state of Washington. He married this good-looking woman, and has three kids. The whole pie, he's got it all. But since that day, that day he left, he's never spoken to his mother. Never even gone back to the state. And she, my Aunt Carol, all she does is drink. She lost her job and ended up waiting tables at the Sizzler." The End.'

Claire laughed. 'How'd you remember a story like that? You make it up?'

'Yeah,' I said and smiled. 'Some of it's true, but most of it's not. They just come to me.'

'It put me in a good mood, Frank.'

'It always does. It's a sad story, but for some reason it always puts people in a good mood.'

Claire got up and cleared the table. She stacked the dishes in the sink and I helped her wash them.

'I'm gonna take the day off,' she stated when we'd finished.

'What are you going to do?' I asked her.

'I thought I'd get dressed and walk down and play the nickel slots at the Holiday and then maybe go see a movie. What about you?'

'I think I might just go back to bed and try to knock off for a couple more hours,' I said and headed for the door.

'We'll both end up all right, Frank, don't you think?' she said softly and tried to smile.

'I hope so,' I told her and then went up the two flights of stairs to my room.

17

THAT NEXT DAY I WENT DOWN to the library and looked
through the newspapers for articles about the kid. There were only
two small pieces on it that I could find. One said an unidentified
male juvenile was left dead across from Saint Mary's, and the other
mentioned his full name as Wes Johnson Denny and said they had
found his bent bicycle on Fifth Street and suspected a hit and run.
They had a quote from his father, Roger Denny, saying how upset
his family was, how horrified they were that someone would hit
their son and just leave him. The article finished by saying there
was an ongoing investigation but no suspects had been found.

I went upstairs to where the phone books were and found an
address for Roger Denny on Seventh Street. I wrote it down on a
scrap piece of paper and left.

The day outside was cold. There were gusts of wind and clouds
coming in. I put my hat on and zipped up my coat and headed

towards Seventh Street. I didn't know what I'd do exactly, when I got there I mean, but at least I'd walk by and see where he lived, what kind of house it was.

When I came to the address I stayed on the other side of the road. I stopped for a time and just looked at it. It was small, probably built in the thirties or forties, painted dark green with white trim. There was a swing set in the front yard and a couple cars in the carport on the side of the house. A mini-van and a red work van that read 'Westside Plumbing' in white bold letters. I don't know why I kept standing there, but I did. And after a while I could just about see the kid and his life there. All the things he did on that lawn, how he left the front door every day for school, and how his mom probably yelled out the window for him when it was time for him to come in. Who knows why he was riding his bike home that night? With no coat or hat on. Not stopping for stop signs or lights. A kid in a blind hurry.

I sat down on the curb and waited. I can't remember how long I sat there, but eventually a man came out with two daughters. He was carrying one and one trailed behind him. He put the one in his arms in the mini-van, in a car seat, and strapped her in. The other was bigger and he sat her in the back seat and buckled her up. He started the car, probably to warm it up, and then went back to the entryway where a woman stood waiting for him. I was pretty far away, but I could tell she was the mother. She was a thin woman with short blonde hair, dressed in jeans and a sweatshirt. The man went to her, he kissed her on the forehead, then kissed each cheek, and then kissed her on the lips. He got in the mini-van and she stood there for a little while before turning back inside.

I got up and left. It was almost dark by then. I bought a six-pack of beer and began walking through the alleys and side streets. I'd stop and sit down on the pavement, near someone's garage or backyard, and open a beer and drink it.

I was maybe a half-mile from the hospital when I passed a house scattered with junk cars that covered the backyard of the place. They were all muscle cars, most up on blocks and parted out. There was also a dog tied to a metal rail on the back porch of the rundown old house.

I couldn't tell what kind of dog it was from where I stood, but I could hear it whining. It was under fifteen degrees. There were no lights on in the place either. All there was was a new pickup truck parked by the alley fence and a couple of motorcycles on the sidewalk.

I stood there for a long time watching the dog. It wasn't doing anything but whimpering. I walked closer to get a better look. It was black or at least dark brown, and it was skinny, mid-sized.

I took a good drink off my beer, and not knowing what else to do, decided I'd set it loose.

I put my bag of beer on the ground and started stretching. I retied my shoes and began doing jumping jacks. It struck me then that I hadn't run more than twenty yards in years.

Maybe I was just too drunk to know better or maybe it was the sound it made, but I went up to the gate, opened it, and stepped into their backyard. The dog was still standing there, still moaning quietly.

I walked up to the back porch and petted it, and it started licking my hand. It was held by a rope to its collar. The rope was tied in a knot that I couldn't undo. The dog was licking my face at this

96

point, and I was trying to pull his collar over his head, but it wouldn't come. I went back to the knot, but I was drunk and my fingers began to freeze up in the cold. I put my hands back in my pockets and warmed them and went at the knot again. After three or four tries I got it. I picked up the dog, and started running for the street. The dog wasn't doing anything, just sitting there in my arms looking at where I was going.

Once out of the yard and into the alley, I put him down, grabbed the beer, and we ran for a while. A block or two away I stopped and petted him. Then I started walking again and the dog followed me. I could see the hospital from where I was and decided I'd hit a mini-mart again before I went to see Jerry Lee.

When I came out of the store the dog was sitting by a trash can. I sat down on the sidewalk and the dog came up to me. I had a pint of milk for my stomach, and when I saw him looking at me I just opened the carton so he could stick his tongue inside, and put a Ding Dong on the ground. He ate it so quickly I gave him half of my burrito too.

Under the fluorescent lights of the mini-mart I looked the mutt over. He was so scrawny and thin you could see his ribs. It looked like he hadn't eaten in weeks, and his fur was matted in clumps all over. But even then he seemed like a good dog, he wasn't mean and he never growled, he just tried to lick my face.

I didn't know what to do with him once I got to the hospital, so I sat down on the steps of the front entrance and petted him for a little bit.

'If you're still here when I get back,' I told him, 'I'll keep you, if you want me to.'

The dog wagged his tail some then just laid down next to me, and when I got up off the steps to go in, he didn't move an inch.

It was past visiting hours, but I made it in without anyone noticing. The room was full. Each bed taken by an old man. Three old guys and my brother, Jerry Lee. They were all watching TV or trying to sleep. I said my hellos to the ones awake and sat down in a chair next to my brother.

He was watching a movie with George Kennedy and an out of control airplane. Charlton Heston was in it. A whole bunch of other famous people too. Everybody was sure they were going to die, and most likely it seemed they would.

'Will you come closer, Frank? I got something I got to say that I don't want anyone else to hear.'

I moved closer to him. I put my ear right next to his mouth.

'Did you find out anything about the kid?'

'Nothing much,' I whispered in his ear. 'His name was Wes Denny. He lived in a house, some sorta foster place, I think. I talked to a guy who knew him. Said his folks died in a car crash, that he'd been shuffled between homes his whole life. No one really gave a shit about him, it sounds like.'

Jerry Lee began crying.

'For real?'

'Yeah,' I said.

'You ain't making it up?'

'No,' I said, 'he was like us. He didn't have nobody left.'

'That makes me so damn sad,' Jerry Lee said. 'I hate myself, Frank. I ain't done anything with my life.'

'That ain't true. You done a lot of things.'

'Like what?'

'A lot of things.'

'No, I haven't.'

'You can draw.'

'That doesn't mean shit.'

'You're my brother and you took care of me. We're just starting our life, we don't have to have done anything great yet.'

'What's a kid doing riding his bike home in a snow storm with no coat?'

'Probably the same thing we were doing by trying to catch that train that night. Just being a kid.'

'I bet I'd have liked him,' Jerry Lee said.

'It ain't your fault.'

'But it feels like my fault, and it always will.'

When I looked at him I wanted to say something to help him out, to ease his mind, but there was nothing I could think of. Maybe there was nothing anyone could say. I saw the kid in the back seat, with his bent legs and arms, all day long. I knew it would haunt me. I knew I'd always think about it, and always see that image.

'Did I tell you that I might have us a dog?' I finally said a while later.

'No shit?' Jerry Lee said and wiped the tears from his eyes. 'Where'd you get it?'

'Stole it out of some guy's yard. It was freezing, chained up, skinnier than hell, probably would have frozen to death.'

'No shit? What kind?'

'Some sort of mutt. He's black mostly. I think I'll keep him if he's still waiting around outside. If he's there, I got to figure out a way to get him in my room.'

'That's good,' Jerry Lee said and tried to smile. 'We always wanted a dog, and now we finally got one. Damn, I guess that's something, hunh?'

'I hope so.'

'Hey, you mind getting my stuff out of my room? My rent's up tomorrow and I don't have any money and I don't need a place for a while. You mind keeping my things at your place?'

'No.'

'Get all the pictures off the walls, okay?'

'I will.'

'Don't bend them.'

'I won't.'

'My keys are in the drawer next to the bed.'

I went to the cabinet and took them.

'You should go downstairs and get the dog before he leaves.'

'I will,' I said and stood up.

'And remember not to go near the neighborhood you took him from. Don't go near that goddamn house with him.'

'I ain't an idiot,' I told him and left.

18

WHEN I WALKED OUTSIDE the hospital and into the cold, black night, the dog was there sitting on the frozen grass in the front court-yard. I ran up to him and petted him and was glad he was there.

I stopped at a twenty-four-hour grocery store on the way home and bought a new collar, a sack of food, and a pint of whiskey. I began walking again but took side streets and eventually sat down on a curb and began taking long pulls off the bottle. The next thing I knew the dog was licking my face. It was morning, near dawn. My head was pounding. I was shaking, I was so cold. I was still drunk but glad I hadn't frozen to death.

I finally stood up and then I got sick and it was full of blood. My stomach was burning. I leaned on a car, picked up the dog food, and tried to walk but I couldn't.

The sun was trying to break through, but it was so cold it didn't seem to matter. I couldn't stand up. I opened the dog food, and poured some on the sidewalk. The dog began eating. I took the pint bottle out of my pocket and laid it down in the road.

When I was able to get up, I crossed the street and finished the walk to my place. We weren't allowed pets in the Morris, but there was no one around so I left the food in the alley, put my coat over him, picked him up, and carried him up to my room.

Once inside I shut the curtains, turned on the radio, and quickly undressed. I put on my electric blanket and crawled in my bed to warm up. After a while, once the shivering eased I called for the dog, and he jumped up and lay on the bed next to me. I felt horrible, my feet were numb from the cold and my stomach was raw and sick. The room spun, and I was sure I'd be sick again.

As I lay in the darkness, with the daylight only slipping through here and there, I began hopelessly thinking about Annie James again. I can't explain why I thought of her then, but I did, and I always hated it when she came into my mind when I was sick and hurting. Because it was always then that the bad times we had had came back to me. When I felt low or was sick with a fever or a bad hangover those thoughts wouldn't leave me alone.

Back when it happened, we had moved for a time, Jerry Lee and I, to the old Mizpah Hotel, an old brick building built in the early nineteen hundreds. We had a room overlooking Lake Street. From there you could see Harrahs, the huge high-rise casino, and the Santa Fe Hotel, the best Basque food place in town. You could also just make out the beat-up train station that was mostly closed and we were just down the street from the Reno Turf Club, where the local men go to bet on sports and horses.

Annie James and her mother were still living at the Sutro on

Fourth Street, but by then we'd been going out for nearly a year, and most of her things were at my place. She spent almost every night with us, with me. The time I was thinking about, right then, it was near spring and she was in her senior year.

We had planned to move in together. Once she was done with school and could get a job, she and I were going to rent a place off Wells Avenue. It was half of a dilapidated duplex. A guy I worked with was living there, and was moving out at the end of June. Jerry Lee and Tommy Locowane had just gotten a house together with another guy, Gil Norton.

It's hard to explain this or, I guess, even to admit what happened. But just so you know, I never got sick of being with her. I would have married her. I know I'm young but I would have. I would have had kids with her too, even though a person like me probably shouldn't have a kid. But I would have if she'd wanted. At night, if Jerry Lee wasn't around we'd lay naked under the covers. I'd lay on top of her and she'd talk to me, tell me how much she liked me, how much she loved me. She'd do all this while we did it. I never got tired of it. You hear guys like Tommy or this guy I used to work with, Mitch Harrison, and they'd always say being with the same girl was boring. But it was never like that with me. It wasn't like that at all.

When it was summer we'd go down to the Truckee River, and in the evening just after dusk we'd find a deep pool and go swimming together. We could see the city around us, all the people and traffic, the casino lights and noise, but it was like we were all right, that everything was okay, that we were the only two people that mattered, that could see how beautiful the lights of the city were.

Nothing changed between us for a long time, I mean nothing went bad. Almost a whole year we were together. It was the best I'd felt since my mother died, maybe the best I'd ever felt.

Then one night I walked down Fourth Street to the Sutro to find her. It was just an ordinary night with nothing much going on. It was a warm evening and not a cloud over the whole city. Jerry Lee and I were supposed to go camping with Tommy and his uncle up in Dog Valley, but the plans fell through so we just stayed at Tommy's, ate dinner with him and his aunt and uncle, and then left.

Jerry Lee and I went back to the Mizpah. We were watching TV for a long time, then I got up and decided I'd walk down to the Sutro to see what she was doing.

When I got there I could hear music inside and people laughing. I could hear Annie and her mother. I could hear a man's voice. I didn't think much of it. I beat on the door and her mom yelled, 'Is that you, Darrel? You back already?'

I didn't say anything. I don't know why, I guess I just figured she'd open the door anyway, and when she did, she was standing naked, and behind her was a man, an older man, and he was also standing naked. In front of him, on her knees, only wearing black panties, was Annie.

I couldn't believe what I was seeing. The middle-aged guy. The TV on with the sound off, the radio playing. Her bare knees on the worn out carpet. The painting of a cowboy hanging on the wall behind her. The bathroom door open. I just stood there. Her mom didn't say anything either, she just sorta stood there too.

'Who the fuck is that?' the man said.

Annie stopped and looked around. When she saw me her face

104

just fell. Her whole body did. I looked at her for a second or two, and then I turned and ran away.

I didn't go home that night. I tried to walk around, but I couldn't even make a block without crying. I just wanted to die, to drown myself in the river. To disappear or jump off the Cal Neva or the Fitz and feel my body hit the pavement. I wanted to get into a fight and kill somebody with my fists or have somebody beat me so bad that I'd just lay in an alley and die.

I walked all through town, up and down the neighborhoods, and finally when I got too tired to keep going I ended up sleeping in Idlewild Park underneath a tree. I curled up tight and fell asleep for a couple hours.

But morning didn't make anything better. The moment I woke I saw her like that, kneeling on the worn out carpet with that look on her face. I felt like that image would never leave me. That it would never go away, like a tattoo, like a scar.

I didn't go to my job. I called in and told them I was sick, and then I went back to our room. Jerry Lee was at work and I lay on my bed and cried.

It was still morning when she came to my door. I let her in and fell back on my bed. I could barely breathe, my breath so tight it felt like someone was sitting on my chest. Like a horse was laying on me.

She was dressed in jeans and a T-shirt. When I looked at her, you could tell she'd been crying herself, her face all swollen and red.

'I'm sorry,' she said.

'I don't care,' was all I could get out.

'I hated doing that, what you saw. I did, I really did. It wasn't my fault. It wasn't. You don't know what it's like. My mom, she owed this guy a whole bunch of money, and he said he was gonna kill her, so that's what I had to do so she could pay him off. My mom used to make me sometimes. I don't do it anymore. I used to, when I was younger I had to. She knew I was moving in with you and she knew she couldn't get me to do it anymore. She said I had to pay her back. She said she'd get killed if I didn't help. I swear, she made me.'

'You're a fucking hooker,' I said to her. 'Like your mom, you're just like her.'

'I am not,' she said and began sobbing. 'You take that back, Frank Flannigan. I'm not like her.'

'How can you say that?' I said.

'I love you, Frank, I swear I do. I've never been with anyone 'cause I wanted to. Not until I was with you. I swear. I ain't a hooker, I swear I'm not. I'm not like that at all. I want to be a good person. I want to be with you. I don't look at anyone else, I don't want anyone else. What happened was different. You don't know what it's been like with her and me. You don't know.'

'What should I think?' I said. I couldn't sit up. It was like I was tired but jittery all at the same time.

'I don't know,' she said.

'I can't believe you'd do that,' I said.

'I don't have anyone besides you,' she said. Her voice was falling apart. She was beginning to hyperventilate from crying. 'I know I'm a bad person, but I can be good. You know I can. And you don't know what it's like with her. It's been that way my whole life. Don't take us away. If you do, I don't know what I'll do. I'll probably just die.'

'You should've just left with me if you had to do stuff like that. When she asked you, you should have. You stay over here all the time anyway. You always say you're gonna move in, but you never do.'

'I know,' she said. She paused and wiped her eyes. She got up and went to the bathroom and blew her nose. She stood in the door. 'I was scared. She went on and on about all the things she'd done for me, and how that guy you saw was gonna kill her. He really did say he was gonna kill her.'

I sat up on the bed. 'I don't think I can see you anymore.'

She began crying harder. She fell to the ground. 'Please don't, Frank. I won't ever go back there. I won't ever. I'll leave everything I own there. I'll do whatever you say.'

'Then leave,' I said.

'You can trust me, I swear I can be good. You've seen me. I try hard. I've been good to you.'

But every time I wanted to forgive her, the image with that guy came in my mind.

'Leave me alone.'

'Don't make me, Frank, please don't make me.'

I got up off the bed. I looked at her, and just looking made me want to die and to kill her all at the same time. It really felt like that. I put on my shoes.

'I'll walk you out,' I said.

'No,' she said, still crying. 'Please don't do this, please. I can't lose you. Really, Frank, don't. I can't go back there. I want to be with you. I swear to God I do.'

She curled into a ball on the floor begging me not to make her go.

I remember I got her to her feet and made her leave. I told her I'd bring her stuff by later, in the next couple of days, but that I didn't want to see her anymore. The last thing I told her was that she was a hooker. That in my mind she was now just a prostitute. I stood there in the hallway of the Mizpah and said it to her, just like that.

She was leaning against the hallway, crying. Her eyes red, her nose leaking, and tears everywhere.

'Don't,' was all she said. Then I went back into my room, shut the door and locked it.

Jerry Lee came in that night but I couldn't tell him what had happened. I just lay there, sleeping a little here and there, mostly I just felt ruined and exhausted. When I'd get to sleep it was bad. Tossing and turning, and waking with the shakes. The next morning I called in sick again. Jerry Lee and I went down to the Golden Nugget and had breakfast, and I walked him to work.

I spent most of the day at the river, and by the end I decided to try to talk to her. That I would go to her place and see what she said.

When I got to her room, though, it was empty. The curtains were open and I could see all their things were gone. I went to the manager and he said they had checked out that morning, the two of them, but he didn't know where they'd gone.

19

THE NEXT MORNING I wrapped the dog in my coat and carried him down to the street so no one would see him. It was going to snow again. The temperature was dropping. We went all the way down Virginia Street to Landrums, the old lunch counter which sat only eight people. I got bacon and eggs, saving the bacon for the dog, who waited outside underneath the bus bench. I got a coffee to go and drank it to keep warm as we walked towards Jerry Lee's old room. I took side streets so the dog could walk on lawns.

When we made it back downtown I walked past the El Cortez Lounge, and as I did so, Al Casey came running out. I was across the street from him, and when the traffic cleared, he made his way over.

'Jesus, Al, what happened to you?'

He was dressed in an orange jogging suit and his face was swollen with two black eyes, his nose was bent and bruised, there was dried blood around his nostrils, his lips were cracked and covered with Vaseline. There was a bandage on his head.

'Damn, I'm out of shape.' He bent over to catch his breath. 'Where you going?'

'To my brother's place. What the hell happened to you?'

'I was walking home the other night after I'd rented a movie and a couple of these redneck bastards were waiting outside that gay bar on Virginia. The one with numbers on the outside. Near the vegetarian joint. Anyway, they called me a queer, and pushed me down and kicked the shit out of me in that parking lot across the street. I don't know why they did it. I thought I was gonna die. It was that bad. Finally I just curled up in a cannonball and tried to wait it out. All because I was wearing a light green suit and walking by that place. I didn't even know who the fuck they were, I'd never seen them in my life. My question is, why would you want to beat up a guy just for walking down the street? It was just terrible, Frank. And guess what movie I was renting?'

I shook my head.

'*Chitty Chitty Bang Bang*, for Christsakes. It was Saturday and I felt like being in a good mood. You know? And they stole the movie. I remember one of them picked it up and looked at it, then just took it.'

'Jesus,' I said. Al was drunk, and blood from his nose began to drip on his suit.

'Your nose is starting up.'

'I'm a fucking mess,' he said. He took a napkin from his pocket, tore a small piece from it, rolled it with his fingers and stuck it in his nose. 'Guess where I'm going?'

'Where?'

'You know Darren Hofchek?'

'I don't think so.'

'He's a guy who used to work at the pawn shop with me. The tall son of a bitch. Got the overbite.'

'I've seen him, I think,' I said.

'Well, somehow he got two weeks in a condo up at Heavenly. You can ski right to your room. Free tickets and free lodging. We're leaving tonight. Can you imagine that? Me as fucked up as I am, skiing down the fucking mountain. With the black eyes and the nose. I won't be getting any ladies on this trip.'

The napkin in his nose fell out and dropped to the ground.

'Jesus,' he said, 'I guess I'm leaking pretty bad.' He took the napkin from his pocket again and shoved another piece into his nose.

'Whose dog is that?' he asked.

'Mine,' I said.

'It's a good looking dog,' he said.

'Thanks,' I said.

'Well, tell your brother hello, and I'll see you when I get back. I'd like to stay and talk but it's colder than fuck out here, and I got a game of gin going inside. I'll see you in a couple weeks. Tell your brother to hang in there.'

'I will,' I said, and with that Al disappeared back across the street and into the El Cortez.

Jerry Lee's room was at the Rancho Sierra Motel on Fourth Street. It was on the good side of Fourth, near the Gold Dust West Casino, near the Gold n' Silver.

Inside, it was like any other motel room, but his bed was made and his room was neat. His shirts were hanging in the closet and the rest of his clothes were folded and kept in the drawer. He kept his things like that, clean and in order and put away.

Along the walls of the room were sketch drawings he'd done. Most were done in pencil or charcoal. One wall was covered with pictures just of motel signs, small ones the size of a piece of binder paper. The Mizpah, the Morris, the Chalet, the 777, Heart of Reno, the Sandman, the Ox-Bow, the Americana, the Ho Hum, the Horseshoe, the Riverhouse, the El Cortez, the Shamrock Inn, the Star of Reno, the Grand, the Rancho, the Austin Arms, the Keno Motel, the El Ray, the Town View, the Windsor, the Olympic, the Ace, the Cabana, the Reno Royal, the City Center, the In-Town, the Stardust, the Sage, the Fireside, the Roulette, the White Court, the Thunderbird, the Monte Carlo, the Sutro, the Lucky, the Desert Sunset, HI-WAY 40, Everybody's Inn Motel, the Mid-Town, the 7/11, the Down Towner, the Reno Riviera, the Heart O' Town, the Golden West, the Uptown, the Savory, the Flamingo, the Coach, the Shamrock, the Aspen, the Gold Key, the Wonder Lodge, the Time Zone, the Horse Shoe, the Mardi Gras, the Capri, the Castaway, and the Fireside Inn.

Most of those are within a mile of downtown, and most aren't even real motels anymore. Once they were new and held vacationers and honeymooners from all over the country, and now they barely survive as residentials. And the people that stay there, they're on the slide too. They get worse as the buildings do.

Above his bed there were sketches of women, most naked, some looked like showgirls, others had tattoos, some were riding bikes, one girl was parachuting. My favorite was a huge picture of naked girls playing baseball.

On the wall behind the TV were drawings of cowboys and

Indians. In some they were fighting and there was blood and guts everywhere and in others they were all just sitting around a fire. There were a lot of drawings of a woman he named Marge. Jerry Lee called her his wife. He had drawings of her swimming in the river, or sleeping in a bed, or laying in a bathtub. There was one of her water-skiing and another of her trap shooting. She was real good looking, and she was peaceful and calm, and you could tell just by looking at her that she was a nice person.

I put all his clothes and things that wouldn't break in garbage bags, and set them by the door. The dog got up on the bed and fell asleep while I took down all the drawings and put them between two pieces of cardboard that Jerry Lee kept for them.

Finally, I was done, and I called a cab and when it came I loaded all Jerry Lee's things into it and had the driver take us to my place.

That afternoon I left the dog once again outside the hospital, in the courtyard, and went up in the elevator to Jerry Lee's room. The room was empty, just him in the same bed alone, and he lay there watching *The Young and the Restless*. He had shaved and his hair was combed back.

'How you doing?' I asked and pulled a chair next to him.

'All right, I guess. They gave me a bath in bed. This fat lady did it with a wash cloth and a sponge. She was sucking on cough drops and had snot leaking down her face but she was pretty nice. It felt all right.'

'You look better,' I said.

'I feel better,' he said.

'I moved your stuff out.'

113

'Were they all right to you?'

'I didn't even see anyone.'

'Good.'

'I got to get some money, I guess, I'm almost out,' I told him halfheartedly and sat down.

'Maybe you could just pick day work. Maybe Claire needs a room painted, something like that. Will you do one thing else for me, Frank?'

'What's that?' I asked him.

'Tommy owes me a couple hundred dollars. Could you get it for me, and when you see him will you see if we can get an extra couple hundred off him?'

'Sure,' I said.

'You still got that dog?'

'Yeah,' I said. 'He seems a real nice one too. All he's been doing is sleeping and eating. He eats more than any dog I've seen.'

'Those scumbags probably never fed him.'

'I don't think they did.'

'You figured a name yet?'

'No.'

'It's a boy, right?'

'Yeah,' I said.

'I'll think about a name,' he said and we fell silent for a time.

'I'm really getting depressed now, Frank,' he said finally, and looked out towards the window. 'I don't know. If anyone finds out, if the police or anybody finds out, will you get me out of here?'

'They ain't gonna find out, but if they do, yeah, I'll get you out of here.'

114

'I just get so damn nervous. The more I'm here the more nervous I get. The TV's starting to drive me crazy. You find out anything more about the kid?'

'No,' I said.

'Poor fucking guy,' Jerry Lee said. 'My whole life seems wrong now.'

'You're just in a black cloud now. It'll pass.'

'I hope so.'

'Things go in waves.'

'I hope they still can.'

'It will.'

'You mind sitting here for a while?'

'No,' I said, 'I got no place to be.'

'Too bad the TV sucks. You think they could get HBO, or at least better cable.'

'I like the new picture of the Indian chopping the cowboy's head off with a tomahawk.'

'I like that one too. How's Marge?'

'She's good.'

'You feel like telling me a story, Frank?'

'Right now?'

'Yeah.'

'I don't really feel up to it.'

'There's nothing else to do. Nothing's on until *Perry Mason* and that's not for another hour.'

'What kind do you want to hear?'

'Something okay, something sorta funny, nothing too much.'

'Well, I've been thinking about a new one,' I said and moved the chair closer to him. He closed his eyes and I paused for a time

115

looking at him. There was a film of sweat covering his face and the faint smell of soap about him, and his hair was combed and still damp.

'Way back a long time ago,' I finally said, 'our dad when he was eighteen got a job as a salesman in a car dealership as a high school graduation present from his aunt. The same aunt in Idaho, I don't know if you remember her, Aunt Bernie. The aunt I already told you about. The one that used to give him *Penthouse* and *Hustler* and *Playboy* for slashing tires. Anyway, she had connections and got Jimmy a job in Reno. He took the bus down here and rented a house and started working. The place he worked was like old Earl Hurley's place. A used car lot. The uncle got him a job working for Ike Linfield, the owner of Used Car Magic.

'He began as a part-time salesman, but within two months he had the top sales figures, and Ike let the only other salesman they had go, so that Jimmy could help run the place.

'Then one day this lady, Iris, walked onto Ike's lot wearing tight black shorts, a red tank top that said "Wonder Woman," and black spiked high heels. She was looking for a convertible Ford Mustang. Ike had two sitting on the lot, a 1962 and a '65.

'So Jimmy walked her to the two convertibles. She knew how to work on cars so she popped open the hood and looked at things, moved some wires around, did a couple other things, then crawled underneath it in her little outfit. When she was done she wanted to take the '62 for a test drive.

'Jimmy went into the office, got the keys to the '62, and said, "The woman of my dreams just walked in. Take a look at her, Ike." Ike took a pair of binoculars out of his desk drawer and focused them on her. He looked at her for a time, then said, "You're learning, Jimmy. Remember, let the words trickle down your tongue like they're the fruits of Jesus." See, Ike was a Jesus freak. He drank and smoked and cheated on his wife, but he also really loved God.

'So Jimmy walked back out to Iris. He gave Iris the keys, she started it up and took them out on the road.

'Jimmy watched her skinny white legs as they pushed on the clutch, hammered down on the brake, and eased into the gas. Iris watched Jimmy as Jimmy watched her. She smiled.

'"You're cute," she said. "Maybe we should go out some time." Then she moved her legs slightly further apart. Jimmy looked at her face. He thought of what Ike said. "Hell yeah, we're gonna. I'm gonna blow your mind, Iris."

'"Is that so?" she said.

'She pulled the car over on the side of the road and just like that, they began kissing.

'Iris bought the car with cash, hundreds and fifties. It was the first sale of the week. Iris had her hand down the back of Jimmy's pants when Ike told Jimmy to take the rest of the day off and spend it with her: "Let Iris take the controls for a while, Jimmy. Don't worry about me, I'm gonna sit back and watch some TV. *The 700 Club*'s on in an hour. Enjoy the rest of the day."

'An hour later and Iris had the '62 up to ninety as they headed east towards the desert. They had brought with them a tub of Kentucky Fried Chicken, a sleeping bag, a tent, and a twelve-pack of cold beer. They finally stopped on a dirt road miles from the freeway. Jimmy ate the fried chicken while Iris stood on the hood of her new car and shot lizards with her stainless steel Winchester .357.

'"You sure are good with that gun, Iris," Jimmy said as she picked up a part of a lizard with a stick.

'"My mother told me the best defense is a good offense."

'"Your mom was one smart woman."

'Iris dropped the stick and the piece of lizard and said, "My mother taught me how to survive in this world. My mother said that each of us is like an M&M in a blender full of ice cream. We all try to avoid getting chopped up. We do most anything to avoid getting sliced, but in the end most of us get the chop and become nothing more than a part of the milk shake. With no difference, no will, all the pressure of the world beating us down, making us like everyone else. But I ain't giving up. My mother taught me the basic three words of life. Good handgun knowledge. And believe me, it really does help a girl out."

'Jimmy threw his piece of chicken out into the desert and lay down on the hood and Iris took his pants off and got on top of him. As they did it she shot the gun over his head and Jimmy said it was the best experience in his life. The way that gun scared the hell out of him made him last for hours.

'The next morning Iris got them back out on the freeway. They were heading to Reno to get married. He had his hands in her pants and she had the Ford up to a hundred.

'They made a quick stop at Jimmy's apartment, picked up his burgundy ruffled suit and bell-bottom pants, and drove on to Iris's house.

'She had a one-room house with a Great Dane/Russian Wolfhound cross named Biff. When they walked in, Iris pushed Jimmy on the bed and took him. He knew then that he'd found something more than incredible, he'd found the meaning to his life.

118

'When they finished she told him she was gonna take a shower and then they'd get married. Jimmy was on the bed drawing imaginary hearts on her sheets when the police broke in and screamed, "DRUG RAID." They handcuffed Jimmy naked to the bedpost while they searched the house.

'They found half a pound of marijuana in a bowling bag, a pound of plastic explosives in a shoe box, an M-16 in her closet, and three grenades under the couch.

'The cops handcuffed Iris and threw her on the bed next to Jimmy. They were both naked. Iris said, "I just picked this boy up, he don't know a thing about what I've been doing. He's just a man I found yesterday, a man who would have changed my life and led me down the path of righteousness. He's the only man that understands me! And most of all he's innocent, goddamnit! Let him go, you cocksuckers!"

'"Fuck you, lady," the police yelled.

'"You think you're funny, don't you? You fucking assholes! A woman has a right to defend herself, and a woman has the right to enjoy herself!"

'As they took her away, Jimmy screamed, "I swear to God I'll bust you out! I'm your M&M, and I'm gonna be the M&M that makes it through."

'She began crying and yelled, "I love you, Jimmy. I love you so deep it hurts. It hurts so bad I think I'm dying. Take care of Biff. You're forever mine! Goddamnit, come hurry up and set me free!"

'Four days later Iris was getting a prison-issue haircut from an inmate when the woman stabbed her five times in the neck. Jimmy had already begun a plan to break her out, and had moved his things into her small house when he heard the news that she lay dead in a barbershop chair with a pair of scissors stuck in her throat. Jimmy was sad as hell 'cause he really loved Iris. Even a year on he was sure he would never fall in love again. It was a hard time, he was sad and lonelier than he'd ever been. And then one day our mother, just out of high school, walked onto the dusty lot of Used Car Magic. He sold her a two-door Toyota, and once again as they filled out the paperwork, old Ike took him aside. "Jimmy," he said, "I think this might be the next gal for you!" Then he gave him a hundred-buck bonus and the rest of the day off. The End.'

Jerry Lee laughed. 'That's a hell of a sad story, Frank, but I like it. That damn woman, she was something. That's one sick picture. With a pair of scissors sticking out of her neck, blood everywhere. You imagine the crazed look in the barber lady's eyes when she was cutting Iris's hair. And poor Iris on a barber chair like that. With some crazy lady standing over you, and you don't even know it. I liked the part about fucking while she's shooting off a gun. I'd be scared she'd shoot me, but it's a nice image. I'd try it. If it was Iris pulling the trigger I'd do it.'

'I might have Jimmy and Biff, the dog, go somewhere next, but I'm not sure. Maybe something to do with aliens. Some sort of man and his dog adventure.'

'Too bad Iris had to die. In my mind she's still alive.'

'I didn't want her to die,' I said, 'but she just did. Maybe she'll come back somehow.'

'I hope so. You know, every time now that you tell a story, the cool girl dies at the end. Always. Never changes. Last time her parachute didn't open, and the time before that she got caught on the rocks and the air in her scuba tank ran out before you could get to her. And the time before that the sand people, or whatever they were, tortured her to death.'

'Yeah,' I said.

'It's 'cause of Annie James, I bet,' Jerry Lee said proudly. 'Hell, at least you've been in love, you know? And no matter what you say, that girl really did like you. All she ever did was talk about you. Marge is the only one for me, I think, and she's just a picture I draw. It sure doesn't feel like love with me and Polly Flynn. If it does at all it's just when we're fucking. I sometimes feel like I love her then. Never anytime else, though. Not hardly ever.

'But then I even felt like that when I used to fuck that fat old lady when we were staying down at the Silver State. Nancy. Even with her, when I had to pay her twenty dollars and she was almost too drunk to walk. Even then when I was about to let go, I felt like I wanted to marry her. I even told her that once. Right when I let go. "Marry me, 'cause I love you," I said.'

Jerry Lee began laughing

'I remember her,' I said and laughed.

'She wasn't much,' he said, still laughing, 'but right then, I swear to God I could have really married her.'

20

I LEFT THE HOSPITAL when Jerry Lee fell asleep. The dog was outside, almost frozen, waiting for me by the entrance. Snow was falling. I stopped at a pay phone and told Tommy I needed to see him and then went to the Eldorado Casino, got an order of chicken chow mein to go, and finished the walk home.

The night clerk wasn't around when I got to the hotel so I let the dog walk up the steps and into my room on his own. I locked the door behind us, turned on the radio, plugged in the box heater, and sat at the small table by the window and ate what I could. I fed the dog a can of food, and when he was done, I took an old comb I had and tried to comb his hair. It was so matted that I grabbed my pocket knife and cut off most of the trouble spots. Then I took off my clothes, grabbed a towel, soap, and shampoo, and the dog and I went down to the bathroom.

He didn't seem to mind much when I put him in the shower.

The warm water hit him, and when it did he just lay down on the drain and licked the tile walls. I soaped him up and rinsed him off a couple times. I did the same for myself, then sat down and let the water run over me while I petted him and tried to figure out what to do.

When I got back to my room I turned on the TV and got dressed. It was not much later that I went to the store and bought a six-pack of beer. I was drinking that and listening to the radio when there was knocking on the door. I called out to see who it was, and when Tommy yelled his name I stood up and let him in. He sat at my table and I gave him a beer.

'I was just at the hospital visiting your brother,' he said.

'I was there a couple hours ago,' I said. 'He seem all right?'

'I don't know. He seemed the same as yesterday and the same as the day before. But he asked me for money. Said he might have to leave town. What's up with that?'

'He tell you anything else?'

'Not really. What's he thinking?'

'I don't know.'

'You gotta know.'

'You won't say anything to anyone? No matter what?'

'Hell,' Tommy said and looked at me seriously. 'You've known me for a long time. I won't say anything to anyone. You should know that.'

'I know,' I said and so then I told him the story. The story of the kid, Wes Denny, the snowy night on Fifth Street. I told him about us leaving, and Jerry Lee burning the car, and the reason he shot himself in the leg.

When I finished Tommy just shook his head.

'That doesn't sound good.'

'I guess not,' I said.

'I don't know much, but what worries me the most is you two leaving. Did you cover it up at work so no one finds out?'

'No, we just left. I was drunk and Jerry Lee was so upset he was out of his mind.'

'Probably looks pretty bad if someone asked around about it. Now you're in trouble too.'

'I didn't think about that 'til afterwards.'

'I don't know what you should do.'

'Me neither.'

'Jesus, the luck of the Flannigans. It's almost worse than mine. I know I owe Jerry Lee, and I'd give you guys the money, but I've been betting the playoffs and I've lost three weeks in a row. I've also been betting my least favorite sport in the fucking world, basketball, and I couldn't even tell you why I'm doing it. I'm down a couple thousand dollars. The most I've ever been down, and to make things worse I borrowed it from this guy, Junior. He's a friend of my uncle's. An old guy. I told him I was going to buy some Russian hand grenades from some military fanatic I knew. But the thing is, there was no military guy and no grenades, and I just took the money thinking I could double it, and then I'd give him back his money and tell him a story about how the guy never came through with the grenades. But I lost the money. Most of it, anyway. I don't know what to do now. If I tell my uncle he'll fucking kill me. I might have to sell my car, I don't know.'

'I'd give you the money if I had it,' I said.

'I know you would. The thing is, when Junior handed me that

money, all those hundreds, I knew I was stupid, but I couldn't stop taking it. I just couldn't.'

'You're starting to sound like my dad,' I said. 'I've never told anyone really, but my mom said he couldn't stop gambling. Craps and video poker. That and betting sports, football and boxing. He lost $3,000 once on a fight. He even went to the state prison in Carson City and was sentenced there for three years because of it. He was a mechanic for a Ford dealership out on Glendale. I think it's still there, at least it was a while ago. It was a small place back then, and he was the only mechanic they had. Anyway, he and the accountant had a system going. My dad would put in used parts. He'd buy them from some guy he knew that did that sorta thing, who sold stolen parts. They'd cost maybe a quarter of a new part. He'd also say to the customer he'd changed things that he'd never touched, or he'd spray-paint the old parts so they'd look new. He didn't do it all the time, but enough. The accountant would bill the customer accordingly and make up fake checks for parts distributors and things like that.

'My dad owed everybody money. He'd gotten beaten up 'cause of it. Someone broke all the fingers in his hand, and he almost got shot 'cause of it. He'd get loans from people and then couldn't pay them. My mom said it was like that for years and years. She wouldn't let him near a credit card or a check book. Their deal was that she'd get every other check of his for the bills so they could get by. When I was little, just a kid, that's when he got caught. Somehow, by somebody, they found out and he went to prison. He owed over $25,000 to people. People he shouldn't have taken money from. My mom said he thought someone would kill him in prison because of it, but they didn't. And when he got out he stayed around for a couple weeks then just ditched us. I don't know where he went but he left and I don't know where he is now. We've never seen him since. So we just make up stories about him, about who we wished he was, but really, he could be dead for all I know.'

'I hope I don't go down like that.'

'I always think that if we didn't live in Reno, he probably would have never gambled. Then maybe everything would have been different.'

'Maybe. I wish I didn't live here, but then I can't think of another place I'd want to live. I just got to come up with $2,000 in a week or so and I'll be all right.'

'Something will come together.'

'I hope so,' he said, 'or I might be moving in here with you.'

'You'll have to wait in line,' I told him, ''cause pretty soon Jerry Lee will get the bed and me and the dog will have to move to the floor.'

21

THE NEXT TIME I visited Jerry Lee the other two beds were empty and he was alone in the room. Just seeing his face as I walked in I could tell that something was wrong. Then he told me in almost a whisper that the police had come by to see him. He could hardly sit still he was so nervous, and when he spoke the words just ran out of his mouth.

'There were two of them, and one asked me what kind of car I had. I got so nervous I could barely talk. But the thing is, they already knew. I told them anyway and the other guy wrote it down. The cop asking the questions was huge with a mustache, a real son of a bitch. You could just tell by the way he was talking that he was. They asked where my car was. I told them it was stolen a couple weeks back. So they ask me why I didn't report it stolen and I just told them that the car was a piece of shit and had been stolen a few times before. I told them how it wouldn't lock anymore and that I use a screwdriver to start it, that it didn't even have an ignition key. It was a real piece of shit, I told them. Which it was.'

'Jesus,' I said and sat next to him.

'Then they told me that the car was found in Idaho. It had been burned and abandoned. They said that normally they wouldn't look into an abandoned car, especially one found out of state, but that the owner of the land wanted to press charges. Wanted to get money so he could get the car out of there. Then they asked me where the car was stolen from and I told them the parking lot of the Sands. I told them I always left it there, that it was just down the street from the Rancho Sierra where I lived. Then they asked me if I knew that someone might have been killed by an old beat-up car like mine in a hit and run.

'A nurse getting off work had reported to them that she'd seen a large old yellow sedan parked by Saint Mary's Hospital. She saw two people moving something out of the car when she passed it.

'They asked me what color my car was. Yellow, I told them. Then I told them that if it was my car the lady saw, whoever stole it probably did it. Shit, then they asked me why I was in the hospital and hell I just started crying. I wasn't faking it, I started crying like a kid and I told them the truth. I said I tried to kill myself but lost my nerve and so I just shot my leg. The big son of a bitch with the mustache kept asking me questions but I couldn't stop crying. Even if I'd wanted to I couldn't. So I guess they gave up. They got my phone number and my room number at the Rancho and left me their card. They said they would come back and just like that they left. What are we going to do, Frank?'

'I don't know,' was all I managed to say. 'They don't know anything for sure.'

'They'll find out. You know they will. You gotta get me out of here. You gotta, I'm gonna go crazy if they come back.'

After that I told him not to worry. I told him they'd never find out. I told him, if they did, I'd think of something.

22

THE TRUTH WAS, I was nervous as hell. I went to the Fireside Liquor Store and bought a six-pack of beer and the newspaper and walked east through the old industrial section of town and down the deserted railroad tracks with the dog following along. I tried to think of what to do and drank three of the beers while throwing him an old tennis ball. I'd toss it as hard as I could down the gravel and dirt that lay throughout the yard, the ball bouncing oddly as it went. The dog would chase after it like a madman.

When I got too cold I went back up to my room. This time the front desk clerk was there and I left the dog in the alley until the fat old man went into the back and then we ran up the three flights of stairs.

Once inside I fed the dog and moved my chair to the window and opened a beer. After I finished it, I opened another, and then the last. The dog moved to the bed and I took a shoe box I had underneath it and set it on the small table. Inside were stacks of letters and pictures. The pictures were of my family. The letters were mostly from Annie James, letters she wrote me after that day I told you about earlier.

They start in Winnemucca, and stay there for a while, almost six months, then the rest are from Elko. She wrote me one a week, every Friday night she said, but I had never once written back.

Sometimes the letters were six or seven pages both sides and other times they were short, almost postcards, written on binder paper, the spiral notebook kind where you have to tear them from the coil. I kept all of them.

In the very last one she said she was living in Elko in an apartment by herself. She talked about the town, the people she'd met, and how her mom and her didn't speak anymore. She didn't have a car or a TV. There was a movie theater near by and she said she'd see any movie that came there, and that she had a library card and spent most of her free time at home, reading.

I looked the letter over a few times then put it back with the others, fastened them together with a rubber band, and put them in the box with the photos, and shoved it back underneath the bed. Next to it was my dad's shotgun. He'd left it at the house when he took off. It was a handmade Remington 1100. I set it on the bed, and for the next hour I cleaned it the best I could then put it back in its case, put on my hat and coat, and left for Tommy's uncle's gun shop.

Inside the store the two men sat facing each other in old gray metal desks which stood behind the counter. Both looked up when I entered and Tommy stood and walked towards me.

'What you doing with the 1100?' he asked when he saw me holding the case. He shook his head and I set it on the counter and opened it.

'What's he got?' his Uncle Gary said and lit a cigarette.

'His dad's shotgun.'

'What is it?'

'A custom 1100 with gold inlays and it has two diamonds, one on each side of the stock. I don't know if they're real, but they look real.'

The uncle got up and walked over to us.

'I don't think it's ever been shot,' Tommy said.

'I don't think it has,' I said. 'At least not much. My brother and I never shot it. My dad owned it, but I think he'd just gotten it when he left.'

'Who'd he get it from?' Tommy's uncle asked, picking it up.

'I'm not sure,' I said.

'I've looked it up before,' Tommy said. 'It ain't on any stolen list that I've come across.'

'What you gonna do with it?' the uncle asked.

'I need to sell it. I was hoping you could buy it.'

'I don't think I could give you the money this thing's worth. You should put an ad in the *Gun Trader* or wait until the next gun show in February.'

'Yeah,' Tommy said. 'This could be worth a lot to the right buyer. My uncle's right.'

'I'm in a spot.'

'I heard about your brother,' the uncle said. 'I know you probably need the cash. I could loan you a few hundred and keep the gun as collateral, and you could take as long as you want to get the money back to me. Six days or six months. As long as it takes.'

'How much would you buy it from me for?'

His uncle shook his head. 'I'd have to check the inlays and look it over, but as is, to you right now, all I could give you is $500, and I don't recommend you do it, that's just all I could give you for it.'

'You could get a hell of a lot more if you could wait it out,' Tommy said.

'I don't think I can,' I said. 'I'll take the $500.'

'It's not the best move,' his uncle said and looked at me.

'I know,' I said, and shrugged.

'Look, kid, I'll buy it from you for five, but I'll hold on to it for a month or two or three. If you need it back, just pay me, or at least set up a pay schedule. If we do decide to sell it, I'll cut you in on twenty percent of my end.'

'All right,' I said.

'Okay,' he said. 'I got to give it a better look over, recheck the numbers to make sure it wasn't stolen, and then it's a done deal. Tommy, why don't you take Frank in the back and give him a cup of coffee and make him take the rest of those donuts.'

Tommy nodded and led me to the back and I poured myself a cup of coffee.

'You guys are gonna leave, aren't you? That's why you need the cash, hunh?'

'I don't know.'

'$500 ain't much to run away on if that's what you're gonna do.'

'We don't even have a car.'

'You could probably pick up a decent car for $400, but I don't know.'

'I was thinking about going over to Earl Hurley's lot. He'd set up credit with me.'

'The only other option is the fight. The Tyson versus Holyfield fight. That's what I would do. Holyfield's gonna win. The odds are good too. That's in two days.'

'Beside Jerry Lee,' I said and shook my head, 'you're the unluckiest guy I know. As far as gambling goes, you're the worst.'

'Look,' he said, 'I know I ain't lucky, but I know this time Tyson's gonna lose. I can feel it, and I feel it more than anything I think I've ever felt. Plus my aunt, she's a worse gambler, worse than me, she bets the football games and the fights and she never wins. Never. Maybe one out of fifteen. She told me she'd bet her house on Tyson. Said she'd bet her whole goddamn life on Tyson. The odds at the Cal Neva are thirteen to one. Probably better now. You read the paper? Everyone's against Holyfield.

'Junior, that friend of my uncle's, the old guy, he called today wondering about those grenades I told you about. Jesus, I know it sounds like I'm trying to work you, but I need your help. I need some cash, I do, or I'm finished. I'm out of a job, my whole future.'

'It's Jerry Lee. I can't think past him.'

'Look,' Tommy said as tears filled his eyes. His voice broke and got shaky. 'I'll give you my car, and I'll get you at least a hundred cash to make the trip with. We'll only bet $400. That'll leave you with $200 cash and a car to make the trip with.'

'You sure about doing that?' I asked him.

'Look, if Junior doesn't get his money back I'm finished anyway.'

'Okay,' I said. 'But I want the keys to your car. Right before we place the bet, I get the keys. I've got to know I have the car.'

'You can trust me, Frank. I'm right,' Tommy said. 'This time I'm right. I know I am.'

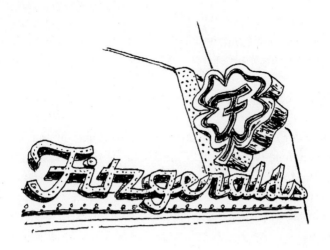

23

WHEN I GOT HOME that night from the hospital the dog was laying on the bed. I poured out some food for him and filled his water. He stretched and yawned and after a while got up. I turned on the radio, put a can of soup on the hot plate, and sat down at my table. I lit a candle I kept and ate. Afterwards, I made instant coffee and opened the sports page searching for the odds on the upcoming fight.

There were two articles I found, both favored Tyson. Holyfield had cardiovascular problems, his endurance was in question, he was too beat up, he was too old. By the looks of it no one really seemed to think much of him. I searched around more and found the Reno odds all favored Tyson. Twenty to one odds against Holyfield a day before the fight.

The dog was restless and so after I finished my coffee I snuck him out and we walked up Lake Street to the University. I threw him the old tennis ball and he chased it down the deserted grass courtyards which ran alongside the college buildings.

I slept good that night and woke early, around six a.m., and decided to go down to the day labor office and try to pick up a job for the extra cash. I took the dog on a quick walk, put him back in the room, made a coffee to go, and went on to the temp office.

I ended up with a warehouse job near the sheriff's station, off Spice Island.

I picked up a ride with another guy assigned to the same place, an old man. The job that day went easy, mostly stacking shipments and putting them in shrink wrap to be sent off. I worked the job that Thursday and Friday. I told the guy I'd be back on Monday although I knew I probably wouldn't be.

When the day of the fight came, Saturday, November 11, I took a bus down to the record store and sold off the CDs I still owned. I took an antique silver dollar my grandfather had given me and sold that at a silver shop. In all, I walked to the Cal Neva with $810.

The sports book was half full and I saw Tommy at the bar with Al Casey and Jim Finer and his girlfriend Diane.

'Jesus, I didn't think you'd make it,' Tommy said when he saw me. 'We only got an hour before the fight.'

'I told you I'd be here,' I said.

'You're a crazy bastard if you go ahead with it,' Al Casey said. He was drunk, but looked better than when I had seen him last. He was dressed in a flannel shirt and black pants. His hair was washed and combed. His face was healing, the black eyes were yellow, and the nose had deflated some.

'I thought you were going skiing?'

'That son of a bitch Darren was lying to me. He didn't have the room, the tickets, or nothing.'

'Darren's a fucking idiot,' Jim Finer said, laughing.

'I wouldn't bet a dead dick on Holyfield,' Al said.

'Shut the fuck up,' Tommy said. He gave Al a look, then turned to me. 'Al don't know shit, Frank, how much you got?'

'$810,' I said, 'but I'm keeping twenty dollars to drink on.'

'The odds are dropping, it's ten to one now. But I still got the strong feeling. Holyfield's gonna knock the shit out of him.'

'You're fucking crazy,' Al Casey said and laughed.

'For once I agree with Al,' Jim Finer said.

'Me too,' his girlfriend Diane said halfheartedly and giggled.

'It's gonna happen,' Tommy said.

'It ain't,' Al Casey said and laughed again. 'Might as well just get a hooker.'

'Don't worry about Al,' Tommy said, shaking his head. 'He's a certified fuck up.'

'Fuck you, Tommy.'

'I'm gonna go bet it,' I said.

'Goddamn right you are,' Tommy said.

I walked to the window and placed the bet. When the clerk gave me the receipt I put it in my wallet and went back to the bar, sat on a stool next to Tommy and ordered a beer and a shot.

People began filing in. All types of people. Most of them men, middle aged and older, alcoholics and gamboholics, casino rats.

Sometimes, in the past, Jerry Lee and me would sit in the casinos, the Fitz or the Cal Neva, and we'd make up stories about any guy that passed us.

'There's one for you,' Jerry Lee would say. 'Look at that sorry looking bastard.' And the guy he would point to was always a sorry looking bastard. Most likely a drunk who gambled the remainder of his life away. Dressed in old clothes which were always wrinkled and unwashed. There's thousands of them. If I was in a good mood I'd say the guy was an astronaut who had to lie and say he made it to the moon when really he was just stuck in a warehouse that was made up to look like the moon. The man was so upset about lying to the whole nation that he fell off, disappeared, and ended up in Reno. Other times I'd say it was a Vietnam vet who was tortured for years and escaped on a raft and made his way to Hawaii drinking blood from the sharks he caught with his dog tags.

Sometimes I'd make him a porn star who couldn't get it up anymore or a sports hero who had blown out his knees or had a weak blood vessel in his brain and if he got hit one more time he'd die or become institutionalized.

Other times if I was in a bad mood I'd say that he'd lost his whole family in a car wreck, or a crazed madman ate his wife on a barbecue while he had to watch. Or that he and his kid were camping and a mountain lion or a cult captured the kid and took him to a cave and he was never seen again. And then the old man spends years alone walking through the mountains yelling out his poor kid's name, and then finally gives up and sits alone at the Cal Neva.

My mind went racing like that through a thousand thoughts before the fight finally started. By then my nerves were completely shot and the odds were down to seven to one. The sports book was full and I was half drunk and nervous as I'd ever been. The commentators on the TV favored Tyson, the people around us cheered him even though he was a rapist, a felon, and I began to lose hope before it even began.

Tommy bought us each a double whiskey and I drank it as the first round began and ordered another. The second round came with Holyfield keeping his ground. The third and fourth were the same. The fifth was the round that Tyson looked like he might be taking the fight. I almost had a heart attack then. I almost walked out.

But in the sixth round Holyfield cut Tyson's left eyelid. They stopped the fight and the doctor looked the cut over and signaled for the fight to continue. The crowd on TV began screaming 'Holyfield' and then with forty seconds left in the round Holyfield knocked Tyson down, nearly finished him. In the seventh and eighth rounds the two fighters tired and stood there clinching each other and it looked like Tyson had recovered from the knockdown. Then in the ninth Holyfield came alive and began to beat down Tyson. By the tenth Tyson was in trouble. Holyfield landed five hard rights in a row and Tyson was saved by the bell. Would he win? COULD HE WIN??? I got so excited I felt like I might pass out. Round eleven began and I could barely breathe and just as the bell sounded the referee stopped the action to look over Tyson's now swollen eye once again. He resumed the fight but Tyson looked tired, he looked beat. Holyfield began a series of punches that all landed. He was destroying Tyson and the referee let it go on for a while, but then, finally, he stopped the fight.

It was the greatest feeling you could ever have.

Tommy and I cheered. I was screaming like a maniac and we were jumping up and down hugging each other. We all kissed Diane, Jim Finer's overweight girlfriend. Al Casey began crying and got so broken up that he went to the bathroom to wash his face and never came back.

We waited a long time, until the crowd died and Jim Finer and his girlfriend left, to go to the sports book and collect the money. When I finally got up there, I was shaking and I could barely put the money in my wallet.

'You get the money?' Tommy asked nervously when I came back to the bar.

'Yeah,' I said.

'Put the wallet in your front pocket,' he said, looking around. 'Jesus, I can't believe it. How much?'

'$5,720.'

'Holy fuck.'

'It's more money than I've ever had,' I said.

'It's more money than I've ever seen.'

'It barely fits in my wallet.'

'We should get out of here, go somewhere safer. You never know what kind of crummy bastard's been watching us.'

We left and walked down Second Street, both of us in good moods, drunk and finally, at least momentarily, successful. We went to the Sundowner and drank beer and whiskey, then to the El Cortez. We got a table in the back and I counted out money and gave Tommy the $2,000 he needed to pay back the old man he owed.

'For once I was right. Wasn't I?'

'You were,' I said.

'Now I can pay off Junior, and now my uncle won't find out. My whole life would have been ruined.'

'You don't have to worry about that now.'

'What are you going to do tonight?'

'I don't know,' I said. 'Probably stop by Jerry Lee's then go home. I'm already drunk and I don't want to get much worse with all this money on me. How about you?'

'Probably finish up this round, maybe get another, and head home myself. I got to work tomorrow.'

'We got lucky.'

'I thought I was cursed.'

'You ain't cursed.'

The jukebox began playing and we each got another round, and watched a group of women at the bar. They were middle-aged tourists, dressed in jeans and sweat tops. They were laughing, smoking cigarettes, and drinking. After a while Tommy went up to one of them, and when he did, I finished my drink and left for the hospital.

The night was cold, and the sky was dark and brooding, and it seemed like it might snow again. I put on my hat and gloves and began the walk.

I stopped by the Eldorado and got him a pint of chocolate chip ice cream and two cookies. Then I walked the last bit to the hospital and made it to his room.

There were two old men in there with him. Jerry Lee was asleep. I whispered in his ear a couple times but he was out. I was gonna shake him awake so he could hear the news, but I didn't. I just found the notepad and wrote:

Jerry Lee,
We won! TKO by Holyfield, 10th round. We have $3,700. I'll pick up a car from Earl tomorrow, but will call to see what kind

141

you want. You know I like Cadillacs, but understand if you don't.
They do break down and suck up gas.
    Your brother,
    Frank Flannigan

P.S. I brought you by some ice cream. Would have left it but didn't
want it to melt. I left you two cookies sitting on the table. I'll
bring by lunch tomorrow. You want Jim Boys or an Awful Awful
burger? I'll call you around 11.

I put the note on his chest and left the hospital. As I walked down
Fourth Street, I could see snow beginning to fall. I turned on
Virginia to walk past the glowing lights of the strip, and I was at
the Fitzgerald when I heard a lounge band inside play the song
'Boy Named Sue' by Johnny Cash. The song is a favorite of mine
and I decided to go in.

   I went past the statue of the Irish leprechaun, Mr. O'Lucky, and
past the rows of slot machines and the people playing them, and
then I saw, sitting at a twenty-one table, Tommy Locowane. I
stopped when I saw him, and my heart sank. Almost like someone
hit me in the stomach and took my wind. I felt sick. I stood there
unnoticed and watched him, watched as they took the chips from
him, and when I left he was almost broke. He was almost done.

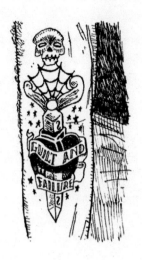

24

WHEN I GOT HOME I opened the door to my place and saw the dog on my bed wagging his tail. He yawned and looked at me, and I felt better that he was there. I took two bowls and set them on the table and dished out two portions of ice cream, one for me, one for the dog. I turned on the radio, and as the music softly played we ate.

The next morning I called Jerry Lee and he told me to buy any car I wished, Cadillac or Toyota, Honda or Ford. The only kind he didn't want was a mini-van or a station wagon.

'Now that we got some dough, maybe you could find that kid's folks easier. He's got to have them somewhere. Maybe they're good people who are sick or something. If you find them you could give them some of the money.'

'I don't think he's got anyone,' I told him.

'Everybody's got somebody,' he said.

'What if I can't find anyone?'

'You will,' Jerry Lee said.

'I'll try,' I told him.

'Maybe when you find someone we could get them subscriptions to magazines. Like *National Geographic* or *People* or *Sports Illustrated*. Who knows what they like, but most people like magazines.'

'I'll try,' I said.

I got dressed, combed my hair and shaved, put on my coat, and took the dog out the back. We walked quickly down First Street, then over Virginia, then took the alley entrance to the Golden Nugget, and I left him there, waiting outside near a row of trash cans.

The counter was crowded and I stood in line and finally ordered a coffee and two orders of bacon to go. Then me and the dog crossed Virginia Street and headed up Lake towards Seventh and the home of the kid, Wes Denny.

When I made it to the small green house I sat a little way down from it and finished my coffee, gave the dog half the bacon, and waited. The red work van I had seen from the last visit was gone, but the mini-van was parked in the driveway, and there were lights on inside.

It wasn't too bad sitting on the cold concrete sidewalk. I still had a little of the coffee to warm me. When it was finished my ass began to freeze, so I took the dog across the freeway to the University courtyard to run us both around. The students were coming and going, but no one seemed to notice or care that we were there.

When the dog had worn himself down we headed back over the freeway, and once again sat and waited near the house. Not a lot of time had gone by when the woman came out with her two small daughters. Once she had put the kids in the car, she went back into the house and came out wearing a winter coat and carrying a purse. She locked the front door, started up the car, and drove off.

The dog and I walked across the street and through the small chain-link fence surrounding the front yard. I found a mail slot on the front door and I took from my wallet $1,000 and shoved it through.

Then we went over the freeway for the last time and walked the short distance to the Walgreens they had just built. I left the dog outside and went in to look for magazines. I went through a lot of them, taking subscription flyers from each that I wanted. For the mom I got *National Geographic* and *Cosmopolitan* and *Sunset*, and for the dad I got *Sports Illustrated*, *Popular Mechanics*, and *Penthouse*. I didn't know anything about kids, though, so I had to pass them over.

We went down past First Street and over the river to the main post office. I went inside and filled out the subscription forms. I remembered their address and a mail clerk helped find their zip code. I got a money order to pay for each as well as envelopes, and put that and the subscription form inside, sealed the envelope, addressed it, and mailed it out.

When I was done I walked outside into the falling snow. I put on my hat and gloves, and the dog and me made the trip up to Fourth Street and slowly on towards Earl Hurley's used car lot.

25

I SAW THE ELBOW ROOM'S LIGHTS in the blurry distance, through the wind and snow, and I knew I was close. Soon I could see the cars and the lot sign and then the office and the shop still standing next to the old bar. I hadn't been there in five years. I hadn't seen Earl or his grandson Barry since the last day that I worked there. It was shame more than anything that kept me away, and as I got closer the memories of old Earl Hurley and the lot came sinking back in.

When he found out I'd dropped out of high school he put me on full time and didn't give me a hard time about it. A year or so later he said if I'd get my G.E.D. he'd help pay for me to go to college. I told him I wasn't sure what I was going to do. Two months later I quit as Jerry Lee and I were gonna move to Montana and live for free with another guy we met whose aunt left him a house up there. But, like they do, the plans fell through and I was too embarrassed to go back to Hurley's, especially knowing how much of a bum I felt for not going back to school.

After that I never even went down into the lot's neighborhood just in case I'd run across them. And the Gold Dust West, where Earl gambled, I haven't been in there since that day, the last day I worked there . . .

When I made it up the steps I could see Earl inside watching TV. I knocked on the door and he waved me in. I bent down and gave the dog a quick pet and left him on the porch and went inside.

'How the hell are you, Frank Flannigan?' he said and stood. He lit an Old Gold cigarette and walked over to me and we shook hands.

'Did I see you with a dog out there?' he asked.

'Yeah,' I replied.

'It yours?'

'Yeah,' I said.

'Well, let the son of a bitch in. A frozen dog ain't worth a shit.'

I went back to the front door and brought the dog inside.

The office was a decent size, there were two desks, both facing the TV, a couch, some chairs, and a wood stove burning. The place was warm and I took off my hat and gloves and coat, and moved next to the stove.

Earl bent down and petted the dog as I stared across the room at the walls and the framed pictures of Dodge Darts that hung from each of them.

'What the hell you doing over here in this weather? I haven't seen you in a goddamn long time. It's been years, ain't it?'

'I need a car, Earl.'

'Today?'

'I thought I would.'

'Has the mutt eaten?'

'Just a bit this morning.'

'I got a bag of food from when I bring in my old dog,' Earl said and turned and disappeared into the back and came out with a bowl of food and a bowl of water. As he set each bowl down ash from his cigarette fell into the water.

'Sorry about that.'

'A little ash ain't gonna kill him.'

'I like your attitude, kid, I always have,' Earl said and smiled. He was dressed in tan pants and dark leather cowboy boots. He wore a long sleeve white western shirt with pearl buttons. His gray hair was combed back; he wore wire glasses, bifocals. He was old, maybe sixty-five or so, but he looked good.

He moved back to his desk and sat down. He turned off the TV.

'It's colder than fuck out there, snowing, the fucking wind's blowing. Seems like a strange day to be buying a car.'

I didn't say anything. The dog was eating, I had my back to the wood stove. It was running hot and felt good. I began to warm, my frozen feet started to tingle, and my Levi's had steam coming off them.

'I wish Barry was here; he'd like to see you, I'm sure. I sent him and Javier to the movies. No use hanging around on a day like today. I can't remember what they went to see, but they went to that new theater downtown.'

'It's a nice theater,' I said.

'That's what I hear. How's your brother?'

'He's all right,' I said.

'Barry told me about what happened. He's in Saint Mary's, ain't he?'

'Yeah,' I said. 'He tried to shoot the rest of his leg off.'

'Jesus, that's rough,' Earl said and took a drink from a coffee cup. 'He drew a hell of a picture of the Elbow Room. They got it hanging on the wall over there. He's good at that. You want any coffee? I made a pot not too long ago.'

'I'll get it,' I said.

'It's in the kitchen, you'll see it all set up, should be some clean mugs too.'

I walked to the back, found the coffee, and made myself a cup, then went back out to the main room and the wood stove.

'Where you working these days?' Earl said.

'Kind of in between jobs.'

'Coffee's good, isn't it?'

'It is,' I said.

'Barry went through a phase where that's all he'd talk about, coffee. The shit that runs through his mind, it's not right.'

'He's like you, Earl,' I said.

'I should kick the shit out of you for that,' he said and laughed. 'But maybe you're right. He's my goddamn grandson, ain't no two ways about it. More like me than Marvin.'

'I've never met Marvin.'

'Marvin's my only kid, lives in Mexico, has for years. Barry bought me a house down there last year. On the beach next door to Marvin. So I been going more. Has everything I need, a satellite dish, a queen-sized bed, an A/C unit. The front room's got a couple pictures of Nevada, even a large picture of the Reno sign at night from the thirties. The son of a bitch even put in a video

149

poker machine so I'd feel more comfortable. Before that I'd go down, but Jesus, I have a hard time leaving the state, and I hate leaving the fucking country. I really do, even for a goddamn week. It's like pulling my own teeth out, but Marvin's my son, so what are you going to do? Anyway, Barry and I fly down there last year, and it's the same old thing, I hate leaving the country and Barry worries about the lot. We end up in some little bar outside of Lareto drinking tequila and beer. All night long we're there, complaining, losing our fucking minds. During this whole time Barry doesn't say anything about anything. We always stay at Marvin's place, and so when we're done we take one of those goddamn Mexican cabs the rest of the way, and when we get there Barry hands me a key. He points to the house next to Marvin's and says, "Earl, I picked you up something the last time I was here." He hands me the key and then passes out on the goddamn road. Just falls down and that was it. Christ, I walked inside and it was like I'd never left my house in Reno. The only thing missing was my dog and my old horse Lloyd, but they say you can't have everything, can you?'

'What happened to Barry? Did you leave him out on the road?'

'What do you think?'

'I don't think you would.'

'You're a good kid,' Earl said. 'You should have been a salesman for me.'

'I'm no good at selling.'

'That's the kind of attitude that can make a great salesman. The key to sales, kid, is making the customer think that you're not trying to sell him something. That you're honest, that you could be friends with them. That's why Barry's so damn good. He'll spend a half-hour talking about women or gardening or sports with some-one, then slowly he eases into the car and then they seem like friends and he gets the sell. You could have a future, kid.'

'I don't know, Earl.'

'Well hell, kid, what kind of car you want to buy?'

'I have $1,500 to spend. I don't want to set up a payment plan or anything. I think I just want to pay cash on it. You got anything in that ballpark?'

Earl stood up. He took the glasses off his face, set them on his desk, rubbed his eyes. With his hands he combed back his thin gray hair and put his glasses back on and stared out into the yard.

'Look at that snow. It hasn't snowed this much in a long time. Been like this on and off for past a week.'

'I ain't never seen it like this.'

'Me neither, and I've lived here most of my life. You sure you don't want to postpone until it clears up?'

'I sorta need the car today, Earl.'

Earl looked at me but didn't say anything for a while.

'I have a couple that might do you,' he said finally. 'A 1985 Honda Civic. It's a good little car, but it's a Civic, small. You look-ing for an around-town car?'

'Maybe something bigger, Earl. Maybe something that you might be able to sleep in.'

'Jesus, that's a fucking horrible thought. I hate sleeping in cars, always have, moving or not. I have a Cadillac. Mid-eighties, but it's a real piece of shit. That whole line is. We got it on a trade. What are you gonna do? I have a couple of Dodge Darts that Barry picked up.'

'Like the kind on the walls?'

'Not that nice, but yeah, same car. Barry's got a real hard-on for them. Picks them up when he can. We have a two-door and a four-door. If I remember right, they both run pretty well. Old lady trades. Barry wouldn't take them if they weren't good.'

'I'd like to take a look at one of those. Maybe the four-door.'

'Two-door would be easier to get rid of, Frank. Kids like those.'

'I think I might need the room.'

'Well,' Earl said, still looking out the window, 'she's out there somewhere covered in snow.' He took a pack of Old Golds from his shirt pocket. 'What do you say we get a quick drink before we go out there and brave the elements?'

I nodded and Earl went back to the refrigerator and came out with two tall cans of Budweiser.

'Look, kid, I'll knock a couple hundred off the four-door if you go out there and start it up. Might need a jump. There's a cart in the shop we use for jumps. You remember it?'

'Yeah,' I said.

'Good,' Earl said. 'It's gold, the Dart, I think it is anyway. It's in the back somewhere. Look on the rack for the keys. I'd get my boots on, but I'm too old to be shoveling snow off a goddamn seventies beater.'

'I don't mind, I'll do it right now.'

'Take your time, kid, there's nothing going on here but the snow.'

It took me a while to find it, it was stuck in the back behind the trucks and cargo vans. It was gold like Earl said, and once I took the snow off, I saw that it had a black vinyl top. The lock was frozen and I went back to the office and Earl gave me his lighter to heat the key.

152

The door opened pretty easy then and I tried to start it, but there was nothing. I went to the shop and dragged out the cart and jumped it with their battery. As it warmed up I sat inside it, and once it settled, it ran easy and smooth. I turned the heater on full, and after a few minutes I could feel it begin to work.

The upholstery was in good enough shape, and none of the windows were cracked or missing, and when I took it for a test ride it ran well. Everything on the instrument panel worked, and even though I never took it over thirty, it seemed like it would ride nice on the highway.

Earl had a bottle of whiskey on the table by the time I parked in front of the office. As I went inside he poured two glasses. The TV was on to a soap opera and the dog had moved to the couch and was asleep.

'What do you think?' he asked. He was staring at the TV.

'*Young and Restless*?'

'*Days of our Lives*.'

'I'll take the Dart.'

'It's old, Frank. Old cars break down. If I remember right, you don't even know what a wrench is. You want another beer?'

'Yeah,' I said.

'Will you get me one while you're there?' he said and smiled.

I went to the refrigerator and took out two.

'What I'd recommend is you buy a Civic, maybe a Toyota. Personally, I hate foreign cars, but Jesus if you need a beater that won't break on you, pick up one of those.'

'I like the Dart.'

'The slant-six is a good engine, but it sucks the gas, Frank.'

'You ain't being much of a salesman today, Earl.'

'I don't know what you're doing, kid, but the last thing I want to do is make life any rougher on you. I'll sell you the Dart, but I'll only take $800.'

'That's a good deal, Earl.'

'We'll see,' Earl said and went to doing the paperwork. I began watching the TV.

'You still any good at shuffle board?'

'I was the last time I played.'

'After we finish up here, I'm closing shop. How's about I buy you a drink?'

'I'd like that.'

'Me too, kid,' Earl said and then lit another Old Gold and went back to it.

26

IT WAS LATE WHEN WE LEFT the Elbow Room. It was still snowing and so cold the snow was sticking to the pavement. We walked back to the lot and Earl gave me twenty dollars to jump an early nineties Wagoneer so he could make the trip home in a four-wheel drive. I got both cars running and left them idling outside the office to warm then went back inside where Earl and I drank whiskey and listened to the radio.

'Don't do anything stupid.'

'I'm trying not to,' I said.

'I don't mean to give you advice, kid, but I like you. It's your mind set, your whole way of thinking, what's bothering me. You're thinking like a beaten man. You have since your mother died. Now I ain't seen you in maybe five years. So for all I know you're smoking cocaine or shooting heroin, but my guess is that you ain't. My guess is you're still an all right kid, my guess is that you're stuck in the same rut as you were when you quit working for me. Drinking with your brother and your friends, fucking around and wasting time. You ain't a piece of shit. You were a good baseball player, you worked hard. Have you had a girl-friend?'

'Yeah.'

'Then you're capable of love. Some broad thinks you're all right. You're not a loser, kid, but if you keep acting like one, then I don't know. All I'm saying is don't make decisions thinking that you're a low life, make decisions thinking you're a great man, at least a good man. And don't be a goddamn pussy. There's a world out there. If you don't open your eyes you ain't ever gonna see it. All right, kid, that's it. That's all I have for you. I got to get home before I get stuck in this shit box. The roads out my way are prob-ably getting bad.'

Earl lived east of town. He had a ranch, a place near Mustang, near the whorehouses. He had a horse and a few acres. He had a porch and a barbecue and a couple dogs. Cottonwood trees and the river. Once in a while, when I worked there, he'd invite us over. My brother and me. He'd let us drink beer and ride around on this old half-blind horse he had named Lloyd. Sometimes he'd even let us stay the night.

We stood up and shook hands. He told me to tell Jerry Lee hello, and wished me luck. The dog was still on the couch and I had to make him get up and leave.

As I sat in the new car I watched Earl as he slowly drove down B Street. The Wagoneer coughing and sputtering, but still moving steadily, and finally fading into the snow and the darkness.

27

BY THEN I WAS DRUNK, drunk enough that I drove back to my
room and packed up my things. I took all the clothes I thought I
might need, and I took all the blankets and pillows I had and
made a bed in the back seat for Jerry Lee. I don't remember what
time it was, but it was late.

I parked out front, in the loading zone, and walked into the old
hospital entrance. I made it to the elevator and up to his room
unnoticed.

He was awake, watching TV, when I got there.

In his room there were two other guys. Both old, and both sleeping.

'Jesus Christ,' he said when he saw me, 'are we going to do it?'

'I'm drunk. Me and Earl went over to the Elbow Room.'

'What were you drinking?'

'Jim Beam and beer.'

'Damn, I wish I was there. What kind of car did you get?'

'Dodge Dart.'

'No shit.'

'It runs good. Earl gave it to me for $800.'

'I'm glad you're getting me out of here. I hate it here more than anything.'

'I don't know if we should.'

'Where do you want to go?'

'Elko.'

'Jesus, what's in Elko?'

'I don't know, but if we go that's where we're going.'

'I don't give a shit, I just want to get out of here.' He moved his legs until they were hanging off the side of the bed, but he was in pain just doing that. Sweat was coming down his forehead, his breathing strained. We took his hospital gown off. He told me to give him the pair of sweats that hung on the chair by his bed. I found them and helped him put on the bottoms. I took his shoe and put it on his foot.

The two old men were now awake. They were staring at us. One guy had tubes running in his nose, the other didn't have anything in him but an IV.

'Those two guys are up,' I said.

Jerry Lee looked over at them and smiled. 'They don't give a shit, they haven't said anything to me since they got here.'

Jerry Lee pulled off the tape covering the IV in his arm and took the needle out. I handed him a crutch, and helped him off the bed, and although shaky, he stood. Together we slowly headed towards the hall.

There was no one around, just the bright fluorescent lights and the hall itself. I found a wheelchair and sat Jerry Lee in it. He put the crutch on his lap. I rolled him to the elevator, and we got lucky, as no one stopped us.

The elevator bell went off, and the doors opened and I rolled Jerry Lee in. When the door opened to the first floor I pushed him to the main entrance and then outside to the car. No one said anything at all. It was almost like we were invisible. I put him in the back seat, opened the trunk, and folded the wheelchair in it. Then I took us out of the parking lot and on to the street.

At a stop light I introduced him to the dog.

'Hello, amigo,' Jerry Lee said and coughed. He reached forward and petted the dog.

I pulled us onto Virginia Street.

'It's snowing like a fucker, ain't it, Frank?'

'It's a mess.'

'Seems like it's been on and off since that night.'

I nodded.

'You know what sounds good? Tacos, you mind picking up a couple tacos before we leave? Jim Boys. Maybe some Mexican fries too.'

'Sure,' I said. 'Did you get any of the antibiotics, or the names of anything you're taking?'

'Shit,' he said and coughed again, 'I left it on the bed stand.'

'That ain't good. We should go back.'

'I don't want to go back. I fucking hate it there. We'll figure it out. We'll call them from the road. They'll tell us.'

'I don't know.'

'They have that oath.'

'They don't give a shit about that.'

'I think they have to.'

28

I DROVE ALL NIGHT and listened to the radio. We were lucky because the roads cleared outside Fernley, and soon I had the Dart at seventy and it handled pretty easy for such an old car. By dawn we were near Elko, maybe thirty miles out. I was beginning to fall asleep and pulled over at the only rest stop I came across. Jerry Lee was out in the back seat, and when I parked I got out and took two sleeping bags from the trunk. I let the dog run around on the frozen grass, and got back in the car, put a sleeping bag over Jerry Lee, got in mine, and closed my eyes.

I woke up three or four hours later with the dog scratching at the car door. It was snowing lightly, the wind blowing. I opened the door and let him in. I fed him the last of the tacos and fell back asleep.

It was dusk when I finally woke for good. Jerry Lee was up, staring out the window. When I looked back at him he didn't seem well, just pale and thin and sick. He told me he had to use the can. I started up the car and drove us as close as I could to the rest-stop bathroom and helped him get out. I took the wheelchair from the trunk and sat him in it and pushed him up the sidewalk.

'I ain't feeling right.'

'How so?' I asked as I got him into the bathroom.

'I ain't sure,' he said. 'My leg, it doesn't hurt really. I'm just so damn tired. Feel sorta sick to my stomach.'

I helped him into a stall and waited until he was done. Then I took him back to the car and laid him in the back seat. I put the wheelchair in the trunk and started the engine.

In Elko I got us a room in a small motel called the Traveler's Inn. It was downtown, fifties style, with an old blue sign, and they took dogs and had HBO. I paid the clerk for two beds then went into the room, turned the heater on full, and brought Jerry Lee in and put him in the bed closest to the toilet. The dog got up on the bed next to Jerry Lee and I turned on the TV and went through the channels until Jerry Lee found something he wanted to watch.

'I'm going to go out for something to eat,' I told him. 'What do you want?'

'I ain't hungry,' Jerry Lee said. 'Sorta thirsty, though. You get me some water, maybe some Popsicles. That trip sorta took it out of me. Maybe if we could hole up here for a couple days, then I'll be good.'

'We got some dough, we could stay here a while.'

'Yeah,' Jerry Lee said. 'I sure like the dog. Makes me want to kill the fuckhead that stuck him out there on that chain.'

'At least we got him now.'

'The three amigos.'

'Yeah,' I said.

'You get me some candy too. Something to suck on. Don't care what. Maybe Life Savers.'

'I will,' I said and zipped up my coat, put on my ski cap and left.

I walked for a long time around the streets of Elko. It's a small western Nevada town that was at one time a cowboy town. Now it's mostly just run by mining. It has a main street with shops and bars and restaurants. It has a couple casinos and is set off the highway and surrounded by sagebrush and hills. It was an all right place, it seemed.

I found a grocery store and bought a TV guide and a package of Popsicles, a gallon of water, and some candy. Lemon drops, Life Savers, and a variety pack of miniature candy bars. I found a row of Basque restaurants and went inside one named the Star and ordered two soups and one full steak dinner to go.

When I got back to the room, Jerry Lee was sitting up watching a movie, *The Searchers*.

'This is a good one,' he told me. 'It's about a girl that gets stolen by the Indians, maybe in Texas, I'm not sure, but John Wayne, he and a couple other guys spend years trying to find her, to get her back. It's his niece, I think, I can't remember.'

'How long has it been on?' I asked him.

'You missed only the first half-hour.'

'I got you some Basque soup.'

'I ain't hungry.'

'You got to eat.'

'Did you bring any bread?'

'I did.'

'I only eat soup when there's bread with it.'

'I know,' I said and handed him the Styrofoam container of soup. I gave him all the bread in the sack and a small plastic spoon.

We ate in silence and watched the movie.

It was near the end when he fell asleep. I left the show on and turned off the lights and got into my bed.

I don't know what time it was, but it was early, maybe three or four in the morning, when Jerry Lee woke me saying that he had to use the toilet and wasn't sure he could get up on his own. I got up, helped him there, and shut the door behind him. I turned on the TV and flipped through the stations until he was ready and then went back in and helped him to bed.

After that we lay in the darkness, both of us awake and unable to sleep.

'All right, Frank, it's story time. I can't sleep no more.'

'What kind you want to hear?'

'Something funny. Set here, in Elko. I don't care if it has women in it. I'm not feeling that way, a naked girl don't mean that much to me tonight. Make it like *The Searchers*.'

'You know in *Star Trek Voyager*, the space-time continuum?'

'I've heard it,' Jerry Lee said, 'but I don't know what it means.'

'See, what happened is we were in Elko, lived here, grew up here. Who knows why or how, but we were. Sent back in goddamn time, that's what happened. You had all your appendages, as they say, and we were more than healthy. I myself could have been on the cover of *Fitness*. We were coming to town to spend the week-end like we would on occasion. We had some dough, and we were well liked by everyone. See, we owned a big old ranch, a huge spread, maybe five hundred acres, north of here. We had a river and hundreds of cattle. We were really damn successful. So we ride in one day on our horses, we only ride ex-champion race-horses, and the dog, he's with us too running alongside. So like I said, we're heading in, but on the way we come across this camp-fire and a group of men. They're on our land. We knew everyone in the county, but these guys we didn't know.

'They stop us, and there stands a guy, a big huge hairy guy with a beard. He looks like Bluebeard the pirate. A cross between him and an inbred hillbilly. He's got a gun and he's pointing it at us. Him and maybe five of his men. Anyway, this black guy's with him, and you and me ain't ever seen a black guy before, and we start staring at him and then the black guy pulls a dart gun out and shoots us both in the neck with a poisonous dart. We both fall off our horses and we're out. Not dead, but unconscious. The horses head back to the ranch to hide and the dog runs off into the sagebrush and waits.

'Anyway, they tie us up, blindfold us, then stick us on a cargo train with some other guys who are all passed out as well. They lock us all inside. The train takes us to San Francisco. We're up by now, but groggy, out of our minds, sick. Maybe five other guys are with us, all in the same situation. Crazy thing is, we know a few of the guys. There's Joe Riley from Winnemucca, there's Pete O'Hara from the O'Hara ranch, and then there's old man Jenkins, the owner of the biggest ranch in Nevada, the Jenkins ranch, the spread right next to ours. See, old man Jenkins, he's been like our father. Our patron saint is old man Jenkins.

'He's taking this ride especially hard 'cause like I said he's old. The worst thing about the situation we were in was, you, me, and Jenkins were to meet for dinner at the Star, then head down to the red-light district. It was our weekly meeting. It was like our church. So we were pissed off, pretty damn upset.

'Well, in San Francisco they put us on a boat, a huge ship bound for Siam. We'd been shanghaied. All of us. They knocked us out again, and by the time we were all up, we were in the middle of the goddamn Pacific Ocean.'

'That's fucking horrible,' Jerry Lee said.

'The crew, they're a bunch of insane lunatics, and the officers ordering us around were even worse. The captain was an alcoholic blood drinker who only liked young boys. He was the son of some admiral and that's how he got his command, but he spent all his time dressing in women's clothes, and when he was in uniform he wore it with high heels and make-up, and his fingernails were painted and he had a talking parrot. The rest of the crew were all addicted to morphine and that's how the captain kept control of them, by restricting their morphine doses. Plus, even though he wore women's clothes and had a fifteen-year-old boy held prisoner in his quarters, he was a mean homicidal maniac. Lethal with guns, knives, and nun chucks.

'Well, we did all right, you and me. We worked hard, kept our mouths shut and took care of Jenkins. We did his work for him and nursed him back to health. It wasn't that lucky for O'Hara or Riley. They tried to take over the ship. They killed four of the captain's men before the captain himself came out wearing nothing but a corset and shot O'Hara and Riley in the head and threw their bodies overboard himself. And you know O'Hara, he weighed about three hundred pounds. The captain was small, not over five feet five inches tall. But he picked up O'Hara and raised him over his head and began screaming bloody murder. He must have held him up like that for a minute or two before tossing him over. Then he stood there with O'Hara's blood all over him, and started screaming again, wiping the blood all over himself. After that we knew our only option was to wait it out.

'Well, months went on, and Jenkins got better. He'd get up each morning and do push-ups. He began working with us. He began eating better and at night we'd sit out on the top deck, and in the moonlight over the Pacific Ocean he'd teach us what he knew. About the cattle business, about his ranch, about his tricks for growing alfalfa. He told us which land we should buy and which we should stay away from. He told us who we could trust in town, and who, no matter what it looked like, would betray us in the end. He taught us how to gamble and how not to gamble. How to drink and not to drink.

'It was like school, and we just sat there and asked question after question and by the time we reached the harbor in Bangkok, he had taught us everything he knew, and we remembered it.

'Well, we were confined to the ship, we were never able or allowed to get off. Then they began to load the ship with new supplies and cargo, and you and me and Jenkins we didn't know what to do. Jenkins was a great swimmer but you and me couldn't swim and none of us wanted to end up like O'Hara or Riley so we just waited for our chance. And then one night the captain brings all these young boys on the ship. He decides to have a party. They roast a pig, they take peyote, they drink gallons upon gallons of rum. It went on for days and slowly you and me slip into the party, kill the crew one by one and throw them overboard. Little did we know a school of sharks were gathering around the boat eating all the bodies we were throwing over, and in the middle of the night the captain comes out of his quarters in a bikini. He orders for the plank to be set out as he wanted to go for a midnight swim. Then he walked out on the plank and did this amazing swan dive, Olympic caliber, into the warm Siam water. Minutes later he was eaten alive by the sharks. After that there was just us, a couple of the crew and the partygoers. The remaining crew and boys were freaked out, but relieved that he was finally gone. They all went ashore, leaving only old man Jenkins, you, and me.

'We checked the supplies and we were full of food and cargo, so we pulled anchor and rose the sails. There was decent wind brewing from the southeast and we headed out of the harbor, and finally into the Pacific Ocean. It was hard going for a time, though. The sea was rough, but old man Jenkins he'd been a captain of a ship before and knew how to get us through it.

'Luckily, yes luckily, we made it to Hawaii, and spent a fine month on the island of Maui recuperating. Our days were with Hawaiian girls swimming in the ocean and barbecuing. Our nights were with Hawaiian girls and parties and dances. The girls, Jesus, they were beautiful and they thought we were the best looking guys they'd ever seen, they thought we were kings. We treated them well and we gave them all the cargo on the ship and told them to watch out for the white man. Old man Jenkins found a load of antibiotics and things like that and we immunized the whole island and gave them all the guns we had. Jenkins would spend long nights with the chief of the island, talking, discussing the future. They set up cannons on the beaches. They formed a militia and learned guerilla warfare.

'When our work was done we got back on the ship and once again headed towards San Francisco and back to the great state of Nevada. But then, Jesus, there was another fucking storm. And what a storm it was. This one was worse than the other, and it took its toll on all of us. Especially old man Jenkins. He got us through it, but the ship was in bad shape as the sails broke off in a hurricane. We drifted aimlessly on the sea for days.

'We ended up off the coast of Mexico. Jenkins was bedridden, worn out, and by this point, I'm afraid to say, dying. He sacrificed himself to save us. We didn't know what to do, and all the dinghies were gone. We could see the coast but we couldn't swim.

'Weeks went by and we spent our time drinking beer and laying in the sun. Old man Jenkins got a little better. We made him rum cocktails as he laid out on the deck warming himself. We caught him huge swordfish and tunas.

'Then one afternoon two guys row up in a dinghy. Goddamn if it isn't a young Earl Hurley, maybe only forty-five, and Jesus Christ, with him is Willie Nelson, and he's maybe thirty and he's carrying that old damn guitar of his. Well, we help them aboard and we all have a few drinks and tell them our story and show them around the boat. We tell them about O'Hara and Riley. We tell them about the captain and the party and the sharks, we tell them about Hawaii and to stay away from Maui unless they mention old man Jenkins's name.

'Well, we dropped the anchor and all got on the dinghy, and Willie and I rowed us to shore. Earl Hurley had a nice house on the beach and we stayed there hoping Jenkins would get better. Earl brought in a couple doctors, but Jenkins was dying, he knew it and we did as well.

'He was too sick to make it back to his ranch so he had us bring in lawyers from the States and he wrote his will, leaving his spread, his ranch in Elko, to you and me. We all sat around him the last couple days. He held meetings with us, final coaching and counseling, preparing us for the life that would be before us. Then on a warm rainy night old man Jenkins passed on, and Jesus, were we sad. Willie Nelson found me in the street with a bottle of whiskey crying in the rain. That's how he wrote that damn song "Blue Eyes Crying in the Rain" 'cause my blue eyes were crying in the rain.

'You howled at the moon and the sea and the sky and drank tequila for two weeks straight. You moved in with a Mexican hooker to a shack by the sea. You'd drink with her and she'd cook and take care of you. And each night as the stars and the moon appeared you'd start up howling and crying. Me and Willie and Earl played hearts, drank tequila, and smoked weed for weeks on end. Then Earl got a telegram and had to go back to the car lot, so he flew out in a biplane. He circled three times and nearly hit a palm tree before he finally headed back to the States.

'Then one morning you appeared with three horses in a desperado's outfit. You were dressed in black, wearing a large sombrero, carrying a gun with an ammunition belt across your chest. "Let's ride," you called to me and Willie. You threw us each our desperado outfit, and we slowly rode our way up north, through parts of California, through the desert of Nevada, and finally back home to the high desert country, to our home, to our ranch. And we called our ranch the Flannigan Jenkins ranch, and you, me, and Willie Nelson would work the cattle and grow the alfalfa, and when winter hit we'd go on the road with Willie Nelson. "On the road again," you'd always say, and then Willie'd laugh and say, "Hell, that sounds even better than when you said it was a Bloody Mary morning. I gotta write that down too." Old Willie, he wasn't famous yet, but he was getting there. And we went all over, east coast, west coast, England, Australia, Greece, and Spain. Then when spring would come we'd be back on the ranch, all three of us. Just working the cattle and growing the alfalfa. The End.'

'That was a goddamn good one,' Jerry Lee said and sat up. 'You think our racehorses made it all right?'

'Yeah, the dog took care of them. He'd drag the alfalfa down from the barn to them and guard them. He got in a death match with a pack of wolves and kicked the shit out of them all.'

'Good, 'cause that was my next question, the dog, I mean.'

'No, he was fine. A little banged up, but okay.'

'I'm gonna sleep to that, to that story. Let's not talk anymore. I don't want to lose it.'

'Okay,' I said and we fell quiet.

29

THE DOG BEGAN WHINING early the next morning so I got myself dressed and took him out. The streets were empty and it was already windy. It couldn't have been much over ten degrees, but we walked around until we found a school where I could throw the tennis ball around for him. He ran hard in the cold, his breath coming from him in a fog before disappearing into the morning air.

He wore out pretty quick, so we began the walk downtown to find a place to eat breakfast. Cars began to appear with more frequency. People going to work, kids probably going to school. I made it to the main street and found a diner. It was crowded inside and I sat at the counter and ordered eggs and ham with a side order of bacon for the dog.

As I sat there I began to get nervous thinking that any of the people I saw could be her, Annie James. When the waitress passed by I thought her face would be Annie's. When someone sat across from me I'd look up nervously thinking it might be her, that she was going to be coming through the door at any time with a new boyfriend, maybe with a family, or even her mom. I was worried about all that. I wanted to see her. Hell, that's why I'd dragged us all the way there, to Elko. Jerry Lee hadn't worked it out yet, but there wasn't any other reason. It was pretty selfish of me, that I knew.

I ate as much as I could, then got a coffee to go, paid my tab, and left. Outside the dog was curled up in a ball near the newspaper machines. I bent down and petted him and opened the sack and dropped the bacon down on the sidewalk.

We walked around some more, went past the Commercial and Stockman Casinos, then past the small industrial section and over the dry and faded Humboldt river.

When I finally made it back to the room Jerry Lee wasn't in his bed. I went to the bathroom and found him on the floor, crying. He was wearing only his underwear and had urinated on himself.

'I tried to take a leak,' he told me, 'but I couldn't make it to the toilet. I lost all my strength and started getting dizzy, so I thought I'd sit on the floor for a bit, but then I couldn't get up. But I still had to go. Now I'm a fucking mess.'

'You'll be all right,' I said. But he looked like a ghost. The bandage around his leg was stained yellow and I wasn't sure what to do.

'Just leave me here, I don't care anymore.'

'Don't say that.'

I went over to him and helped him up and sat him on the toilet and he began crying again.

'I'm a failure,' he said.

'You're just hurt, that's all. You know how to clean your leg?'

'I don't know.'

'It's all covered in piss. I think we ought to change the bandage.'

'I don't care,' he said again.

'I'll go to the store and get that white tape . . . maybe some gauze, hydrogen peroxide. Maybe we could wrap the leg in a plastic bag, and you could get into the shower and clean up. Then I'll get you back in bed and go to the store and get all the junk we need and we'll change the bandage.'

'All right,' Jerry Lee said and wiped his eyes.

'You think you can stand up that long? In the shower, I mean?'

'Maybe,' he said. I took the plastic bag liner from the small trash can in the bathroom and gave it to him. I looked around for a rubber band or tape but there wasn't any, and so I took a lace from my shoe and Jerry Lee put the plastic bag over the leg and tied the lace around it.

I started the water and got the temperature right. A small cloud of steam began to appear on the mirror as I got him up. I took off his underwear and helped him into the tub.

'I don't know how long I can stand,' he said weakly.

I took the soap and washed him the best I could. The water getting me wet and getting all over the bathroom floor.

'You got any shampoo?' he asked. 'My hair smells pretty goddamn bad.'

'Don't think so,' I said. 'We can just wash it with soap.'

I took the bar and washed his hair, then rinsed him and shut off the water. I helped dry him while he leaned against the tile wall, then I helped him out of the tub and into his bed.

He called for the dog, and it jumped up and lay next to him, and I clicked on the TV and went through the channels and found him a movie with Charlton Heston in it, *Planet of the Apes*.

'That was horrible,' Jerry Lee said.

'I know,' I said.

'I'm glad I don't have to get up for a while, that I don't have to take a leak or move anytime soon.'

'I'm gonna go out and get you some bandages,' I said. 'You want any breakfast?'

'I don't know,' he said after a while. 'Maybe orange juice. Maybe get that soup again for lunch. I might be hungry by then. Ask for the bread too. And if you don't mind, could you get me a pad of drawing paper and some pencils? Now that I'm out of the hospital maybe I'll feel like drawing again.'

'I'll get all that stuff. You gonna be okay by yourself?'

'I'll be all right. I think I'll be just fine. I'm sorry you had to see that.'

'It's nothing.'

'It is, though, it really is,' he said.

30

WHEN I GOT BACK Jerry Lee was awake and *Planet of the Apes* was still on. The room was warm and the dog was asleep. I gave Jerry Lee an orange juice and a waffle. When the dog woke Jerry Lee gave him some, and I took off my coat and sat on the bed next to his.

'I got a bunch of stuff, although I'm not sure it's right,' I said. 'When do you want to change the bandage?'

'I guess we should probably do it soon,' he said and looked at me. 'I'd do it myself, but I probably wouldn't do the best job. It's ugly to look at, though. If you do it, it might make you sick.'

'We gotta do it,' I said and went to the cooler and found a beer and opened it.

'Wish I could drink,' Jerry Lee said.

'You will soon enough.'

'Maybe you better have a few before you change it.'

'Maybe.'

'I almost puked when I first saw it. It's an awful looking sight.'

I drank three beers and we finished the movie before I did anything. Then I moved Jerry Lee to the toilet, and while I went for the supplies he took off the old bandage and set it in the small plastic trash can under the faucet.

He was more than right, it was hard to look at, and I was glad I was drunk. But he told me what to do and I followed his instructions the best I could and it went along okay. First I set down a couple towels on the tile floor underneath the leg, then poured hydrogen peroxide over the whole stump and a couple times over the stitches. It fizzed up on them, and I wiped away the foam with Kleenex, then dried it off with gauze. Then I just began wrapping the leg with gauze. I took a couple big pieces and folded it over the front, and taped them to the gauze I'd wrapped on the side. I made it tight, but not so much that it hurt him. It took some time, and I wasn't sure, but it seemed to work out.

After I was done I helped him back to bed. It was almost eleven a.m. by then, and I found him another movie on the TV. I took off my shoes and sat on the bed and drank a beer and began to watch *The Great Waldo Pepper* with Robert Redford.

I crawled into bed and we watched it together in silence. After a time I could hear Jerry Lee snoring. When the movie was over I got up again, opened a beer, and looked through the phone book. I didn't think I'd find her name, I was almost sure I wouldn't, but under the Js it was there. Annie James. It listed her phone number, but there was no address. I sat for a time not sure what to do, so I opened another beer, and then another, and called her. She answered on the third ring and after we talked for a while we set up a time to meet.

When I got there, to the Stockman Casino, I almost didn't go in, I was so nervous. I stood outside for a long while and went back and forth about it.

I saw her right away, sitting in a booth drinking coffee. My stomach bunched up in a knot and I got nervous as hell. I wanted her to still like me, I guess that was the thing. Even after all that had happened, that's what I hoped for. That's what I was worried about.

When she saw me she stood and smiled. She looked the same, although skinnier, and her hair shorter. She was dressed in a black skirt with black stockings and black shoes. She wore a plain red sweater, and no make-up or lipstick.

'Hi, Frank,' she said uncertainly.

'Hello,' I said and smiled at her. I sat down and a waitress came and gave us menus.

'I work at a hardware store,' she said when the lady had gone. 'But I was lucky and I didn't have to go in today. I work in the office. I answer phones and file. Things like that. It's a good job, though. The people are all right. I live not far from here in an apartment. In a studio. It's smaller than any motel I've ever stayed in, but it's pretty nice. It's my own place. I even painted it, and it has a full kitchen.'

'What color did you paint it?'

'The bathroom I painted white, it was dark green, and I painted the front room this sorta cream color, it looks good though. I can't believe you're here.'

'Me neither.'

'I'm glad you called. I really am.'

'I'm staying over at the Traveler's Inn, you know where that is?'

'No,' she said and laughed. 'I try to avoid motels.'

'Just down the street, maybe a half-mile from here.'

'You guys on vacation?'

'No,' I said. 'It's nothing like that.'

The waitress came to take our order.

'I think I'm too nervous to eat,' Annie James said and looked at me. 'If I ate, I think I'd puke.'

'I'll get a piece of apple pie and coffee.'

The waitress wrote down the order and walked away.

'I live by myself now,' Annie said and picked up her spoon and began playing with it. 'When we left that night, left Reno, my mom she said we had to. Said someone was trying to kill her. She was out of her mind. I don't think anyone was really trying to kill her, but I'm not sure either. I was gonna stay, but I didn't know what to do. I thought you'd want me to leave. I don't know, I was scared, I guess. I felt horrible. I hated myself for what I did. I still do. I don't think I could have faced myself if I stayed. I didn't have anywhere to live either and no money. So there I was with her. First we went to Winnemucca, then we came to Elko and stayed with a friend of hers for a while, then my mom got a job working at one of the houses and I found a job as a maid and then I got the job at the Home Depot and when I'd saved enough money I rented the place I have now. My mom she left town six months ago. Met some guy and they went together. I think they're in Texas somewhere. I haven't heard from her much. She calls every month or so. I only met the guy she left with once, but I'm more than relieved she's gone.'

'I'm glad you're living on your own,' I said.

'I still think about you. All the time I do.'

'I think about you.'

'I'm sorry,' she said.

'I got your letters.'

'Jesus, I'm glad you're here,' she said and smiled again. 'Are you gonna stay for a while?'

'I don't know,' I said. 'I don't know what we're gonna do.'

When we left the coffee shop, we left together, and as we walked along the streets towards the motel I told her about what had happened, about Wes Denny and Jerry Lee. About his leg and the fight between Tyson and Holyfield, and the money we made from it. And I told her how I saw Tommy Locowane sitting at the twenty-one table, and how I took Jerry Lee from the hospital.

It was near dusk and we could see our breath as we walked. We were near a street lamp and she held my hand. She had mittens on, and she reached for my hand and I held it and we walked the rest of the way to the room like that.

Jerry Lee was awake when we came in. The dog was next to him, the TV was on, and it was warm inside.

'Holy shit,' Jerry Lee said and his face cracked into a smile. 'I haven't seen you in a long time. I knew there was a reason we came to Elko. I just couldn't figure it out.'

'It's good to see you,' she said and smiled. 'This must be your dog. He's cute.' She went over and began petting him. Then she reached over and began petting Jerry Lee's head. 'Here you go, Jerry Lee, I don't want you to feel left out.'

Jerry Lee laughed and then we all sat on the bed and talked. She told him about her place and her job. How she was taking

179

classes at the community college, and how she had a fish tank and four fish, and how she named them A, B, C, and D.

Without her even asking and without me talking to him, he told her everything, about the guilt he had for the kid Wes Denny, a kid, Jerry Lee told her, who had no family, no one at all.

'It makes me hurt in a way that don't ever go away,' Jerry Lee said and tears filled his eyes. 'I killed him.'

'It wasn't your fault,' I said.

'I guess that doesn't really matter,' Jerry Lee said. 'It doesn't. I killed a kid and now I hardly want to live at all.'

'Don't say that,' Annie James said. 'What would Frank do without you?'

'He wouldn't be in trouble, that's what,' Jerry Lee said and turned his face away.

We sat there in silence for a long while, then I told Annie I'd walk her home. She stood up and went over to Jerry Lee and kissed him on the forehead and said goodbye, then left the room and waited for me outside.

'You're gonna be all right,' I said. I sat on the bed next to him.

His head was still turned away.

'I don't know,' Jerry Lee said weakly.

'You will. You just got to ease up on thinking about it. It wasn't your fault, these things happen. They happen for no reason. It's horrible, but it's not your fault.'

'It is my fault, though, it is. It is my fault because I'm alive. Things happen because of me. Things change and are ruined 'cause of me. 'Cause of my stupid life. 'Cause I'm here on this planet.'

'It's not right to say that,' I said. 'You're wrong when you say it.'

He turned his face to me and wiped the tears from his eyes. 'I'll be all right, Frank,' he said finally. 'I guess I'm just tired. And all this traveling and my leg and not knowing what I'm gonna do are all causing me to lose my mind. I just need to sleep, don't you think?'

'Yeah,' I said.

'I'll be okay in a while,' he said. 'You should take Annie home. You should spend the night if she wants. I'm feeling better than I was. Maybe I just needed to get it out. But really, I just think I need to knock off for a while.'

'I'll come back, you can't even take a piss on your own.'

'I can, I already got up a couple times while you were gone. You should stay if you can,' he said and tried to smile. 'One of us needs to have a decent time.'

31

WE WERE PRETTY QUIET as we walked to her home, but once there she invited me in and we started kissing pretty soon after that. I hadn't even hugged anyone in almost two years. I didn't know what to think about it, I really didn't, but it felt good. It felt lucky. Even so, I wasn't real sure of her yet, so I didn't sleep with her although I wanted to. Mostly we just talked and when we finally did sleep I left my pants on.

In the morning she made me breakfast and I walked her to work. When I got back to the motel it wasn't even seven. It was still cold out, and I guessed it wasn't even in the teens. When I came to our room I could see the window open, the door ajar, and when I went inside Jerry Lee was on the bed in his underwear, with no blankets on him and the heater off. The TV was on, with the sound low, and he was shaking, his skin almost blue, his teeth shaking so much that he could barely talk when I woke him.

'What the fuck are you doing?' I said and kicked the dog off the blankets, which were laying on the floor, and put them over him. I shut the window and the door and turned the heater on full. I took the bedspread and blanket off my bed and covered him. I went out to the car, took a sleeping bag and put it over him as well.

Then I got in bed with him, next to him to warm him. I held on to him to try to warm him, and it was like holding ice.

'Wha . . . are . . . you . . . doing?' he said and looked over at me. He was shaking so hard it was like he was having convulsions.

'Trying to warm you up, you stupid motherfucker.'

'Yeah?' he said and closed his eyes. We didn't say anything else, and then he fell into a sleep. I stayed there for a long while holding him and I fell asleep myself and when I woke maybe an hour had passed and his body temperature seemed closer to normal and the room had warmed. I got up and took a shower and shaved, and as I dressed the dog began scratching at the door. Jerry Lee was still out, so I wrote him a note and told him not to do anything while the dog and I went out for a walk.

We went downtown and over the bridge and once again followed the path that ran next to the Humboldt river. There was snow on the ground, and I threw the dog the tennis ball and he'd run after it trying to find it in the snow. But then I threw it way past him and into the bushes alongside the river. The dog went after it, disappearing into the brush. But he didn't come out and then I heard him start to bark. I called for him but he wouldn't come, so I went to get him and worked my way through the maze of bushes and frozen brush until I came across him yelping hopelessly at a partially snow-covered sleeping bag.

It looked as though there was a person in it, but nothing was moving, and I thought that if someone was in there, they were most likely dead. Frozen.

I kicked the sleeping bag to make sure, and something inside moved, then a head came out from it. The dog began barking harder.

'Be quiet,' I yelled at the dog and he stopped quick.

'You all right in there?' I asked.

The person in the bag got out and stood up. It was a kid, a boy in a parka and jeans. His hair was long, black and stringy. He was dirty and shivering.

'Seems like everyone I know has gone totally fucking crazy,' I said.

The kid didn't say anything, just stared at the ground.

'You all right?' I asked him.

'Are you gonna take me to jail?'

'Why'd I do that?'

'I dunno.'

'Why the hell are you sleeping out here?'

'I didn't know it was gonna snow,' he said. The kid still wouldn't look at me. He was young, fourteen, maybe fifteen at the most.

'It's winter,' I said.

'I know,' he said. He bent down and felt inside the sleeping bag and pulled out a pair of cowboy boots and put them on.

'You a cowboy?'

'No,' he said.

'You sleep much? That bag don't look like it's made for snow. Looks like a slumber party bag.'

'I've been freezing my ass off all night,' the kid said and

laughed in an awkward sorta way.

'You got any folks?'

'No,' the kid said.

'You hungry?'

'I haven't eaten anything but bread and peanut butter for a week.'

'Get your things and I'll buy you breakfast.'

'You ain't gonna call the cops?'

'Have you killed anybody?'

'No.'

'Then I probably won't.'

'If you leave me your address I could send you the money for breakfast when I get where I'm going.'

'Where are you going?'

'Wyoming,' the kid said and smiled and finally he looked at me. His eyes were brown and his teeth were crooked and he had silver caps on three of his bottom teeth.

'What's in Wyoming?'

'A lot of things,' the kid said and shook the snow off his sleeping bag and rolled it and tied it with two pieces of string that he took from his pocket. Then he stood before me and took a picture from a worn-out leather wallet. The wallet was faded black with a white horseshoe emblem on it, it was thin, and from what I could see there were only a few dollars in it.

'This,' he said, 'it's my horse. It's in Wyoming. It's a goddamn thoroughbred.'

'Is he fast?'

'He's really goddamn fast,' the boy said, smiling as he stared at the picture. 'Just look at him.'

I looked at the picture and then the kid put it away, and we began walking towards the road.

The kid didn't hardly talk the whole time we ate breakfast. He only looked at me when I talked about Wyoming or the horse, asked him questions about it, its name, its age, things like that. The kid just stared at the place mat, and when the food came he ate with his head down, shoveling the food in. A ham and cheese omelet, hash browns, toast, a side order of sausage, and a side order of hotcakes.

When we left the diner, we stood out on the sidewalk and watched the dog eat the side of bacon I'd gotten him.

'You really heading to Wyoming?'

'Yeah,' the kid said.

'You a runaway?'

'Sorta,' he said.

'You know anybody in Wyoming?'

'My grandma. She has the horse.'

'How much dough you got?'

'Seven dollars,' the kid said.

'I'll buy you a bus ticket. Where in Wyoming exactly?'

'Laramie,' the kid said and looked at me again.

'I'll get you a ticket there,' I said.

'You don't have to do that, mister.'

'My brother would kill me if he knew you were out there in that sleeping bag and I didn't help,' I said. 'You got to get yourself a better bag.'

'I intend to.'

'Good.'

'If you give me your name and address I'll send you the money when I get there. I swear I will.'

'Worry about that later,' I said and went back inside the diner and asked the cash register lady the directions to the Greyhound.

When I got back outside the kid was playing with the dog, chasing it around in circles. I told him that I had the directions and we began walking down the street towards it.

The dog and him followed behind, still playing, chasing each other around. The dog was barking and the kid was laughing.

Every once in a while I'd hear the kid whisper to the dog. 'You're a good goddamn dog,' he'd say and bend down and pet it.

'You're a really good goddamn dog.'

32

I LEFT THE KID sitting in a plastic seat at the bus station with a ticket to Laramie, Wyoming, and three pre-made sandwiches from a food cart they had. He was already starting in on one as we said goodbye.

The walk back to the motel was short, and I stopped and bought a twelve-pack of beer on the way. Jerry Lee was still asleep when I got to the room, the blankets and sleeping bag still covering him, the heater still on.

The dog moved next to him, so I opened a beer and turned on the TV. I decided then to call Tommy Locowane to see if he'd heard anything about Jerry Lee and me.

I went to the motel office, placed a deposit on the phone, then came back to the room and called the gun shop.

'I ain't seen him,' his Uncle Gary said. 'He's got me worried as hell. I called the cops, I put a missing persons out on him, but nothing's shown up. This is the fifth day. You ain't seen him?'

'No,' I said.

'When was the last time?'

'I saw him at the fight, we were all watching the fight at the Cal Neva,' I said.

'That was when? Friday?'

'Yeah.'

'He hasn't been home since then, since that night. He never came home that night.'

'He was at the Fitz the last time I saw him,' I said.

'I don't know what to think. My wife's in bed sick, she's so worried. You haven't seen anything, heard anything?'

'No,' I said.

'I don't care what he's done, Frank, if you know you got to tell me. You owe me that much.'

'I don't know anything,' I said.

'Was he with anyone different, a woman?'

'No,' I said. 'It was just me and Al Casey for the most part.'

'I got a hold of Al, but he hasn't seen him either.'

'I'll let you know if I hear anything,' I said.

'I'd appreciate it,' his uncle said and hung up the phone.

33

IT WAS DUSK when Jerry Lee woke, his voice raw. He was sweating with a fever. He apologized for the night before, said he was depressed, that he got crazy, but that he was all right now, just felt a little sick. I didn't really yell at him for it. I didn't really know how to handle it, so like I do, I said nothing.

I just changed the subject and told him about calling Tommy and about the kid from Wyoming, then I went out to the Star and bought him an order of soup with extra bread.

We watched an old movie called *Rebecca* while we ate. Jerry Lee got through half of the soup, which I thought was a good sign.

The movie was all right, but Jerry Lee was asleep by the end when the main part happened, when the house burned, and Rebecca was finally killed off. Her name getting burned off that pillow. I don't remember what time after that, but Annie came by the room, and she and I laid on the bed and talked quietly and drank the beers I kept on ice in the cooler.

We spoke as easy as we had before, and finally we shut off the TV and took off our clothes down to our underwear and got in the bed. In the darkness she told me the real story about her trip to Elko, and how one afternoon in the back room of her mom's friend's house she tried to kill herself. She had stolen a bottle of painkillers from her mother's purse and took all twenty-five. Her mother's friend found her, went in the back room and saw her laying on the floor. She saw the bottle and the empty beer cans around her. The woman picked her up and drove her to the hospital.

She went to counseling and moved out on her own and tried once again with razor blades, and in the darkness I felt the scars on her wrists. I held her while she told me, and afterwards she began kissing me. She took off her underwear and took off mine and then laid on top of me. In the darkness we were like that, her tears were mixing with our spit as we kissed and I held on to her as hard as I could. I held on to her like, if I let go, she and me, we'd disappear.

The next morning, when I woke, she was gone and Jerry Lee was already watching the TV. He looked worse.

'You all right?' I asked him and sat up in bed.

'I don't know,' he said. 'I might have a fever or something. I feel sick to my stomach.'

'Probably got to eat.'

'Nothing sounds too good right now,' Jerry Lee said.

I got up and dressed. I looked out the window and it was a dark, gray day with snow just beginning to fall.

'Maybe we should take you to the hospital.'

'I'm okay, shit, I don't want to go back there.'

I sat on the bed and petted the dog and tried to think.

If I took him to the hospital he'd probably go to jail, then maybe he really would kill himself. I went back and forth about it, over and over.

'You know what we need?'

'What's that?'

'A cassette deck,' I said and put on my coat. 'Don't do anything crazy. I'm gonna walk the dog and go get us some music and some food.'

An hour later, as I made my way back, it began snowing hard and the wind was howling and screaming. The dog was walking right next to me with his head down. I was carrying a bag of groceries, a bottle of Jim Beam and a small cassette player, and I was already a little drunk. I'd hit three or four places along the way as my nerves were shot. Why did I bring Jerry Lee? Why did I get him out when he should have stayed in the hospital? Did I just bring him out 'cause I was too scared to come alone? Did I bring him out just 'cause of Annie? Just so I could see her? My mind was racing with thoughts like that, and I was beating the hell out of myself.

FLANNIGAN the BROTHERS

Three High Rolling Hard Going Travelers

34

'FRANK, HEY, FRANK,' Jerry Lee yelled at me.

When I woke I was on the floor and it was dusk. I sat up and looked at him.

'What time is it?'

'I don't know. All I know is I got to take a leak and I don't think I can get up anymore.'

'All right,' I said and tried to stand up.

'I'm about to piss my pants,' Jerry Lee said. 'If I do, I get your bed.'

'I'm hurrying,' I said and helped him up and took him to the toilet. He was sweating heavily, his T-shirt soaked.

'This is the greatest feeling I've ever had,' he said as he went.

My head was pounding. I could barely stand I was so hung over.

'This is the longest I think I've ever pissed.'

'I'm gonna get sick soon,' I said.

'I'm almost done,' Jerry Lee said.

I helped him back to the bed, then went into the bathroom and laid down on the cool tile trying to calm my stomach.

'You all right?' Jerry Lee asked after a while. He tried to say it loudly but his voice cracked when he did. And just then, in that one sentence, you could tell how sick he was.

'I don't know,' I finally said back to him. 'But you sound worse than me. We're going to the hospital tomorrow.'

'I'll be all right,' he said. 'I think you should just drink beer from now on.'

'You're probably right,' I said and closed my eyes.

'Looks like you almost drank half of the bottle. You know Willie Nelson says whiskey's the only thing that almost killed him. More than any other drug, and I'm sure he's seen and done them all.'

'I'm sure he has,' I said.

'I wish we had more than just HBO. I'm sick of it already. Maybe we should get a short-wave radio. We could talk to people all over. People in Tasmania or Africa or Iceland.'

'That would be something,' I said and got up and walked to the bed and laid on it. The dog jumped up next to me and I fell asleep.

It was the middle of the night when I woke next.

'Are you awake?'

'Yeah,' he said.

'How you feeling?' I asked him.

'I'm having nightmares,' he said softly and we fell quiet for a time and then I got up and went to the cooler and took a beer from it and opened it.

'You mind if I have one? It sounds good. Nothing has been sounding good, not even water, but that does, an ice-cold beer.'

I walked over to him with one, opened it, and handed it to him.

'We've drank a lot of beers, ain't we, Frank?'

'I guess so,' I said and sat back down on the bed.

Jerry Lee leaned over to the bedside table and pulled the cassette deck close to him and hit play. Willie Nelson came on softly.

'I sure like him,' Jerry Lee said.

'Me too,' I said.

'Sometimes he can drive me crazy, but sometimes, like right now, there doesn't seem like there could be any better music. You mind if I have a drink off the whiskey?'

'It probably ain't good to,' I said.

'It can't be that bad,' Jerry Lee said.

I went into the bathroom and found him a plastic cup and poured him a drink.

'You think you could live in Elko?' Jerry Lee said.

'I think it could be pretty nice. It's different.'

'What do you think about Annie?'

'What do you mean?'

'You gonna start seeing her again?'

'I don't know.'

'She still likes you,' Jerry Lee said. 'You can just tell by looking at her.'

'I don't know.'

'You still ain't ever told me what happened.'

'You probably wouldn't like her if you knew.'

'I don't know, she's always been all right to me.'

I didn't say anything.

'You ever told anyone? What happened, I mean.'

'No,' I said.

'You should tell someone. You never talk about anything. I know you better than anyone and I don't know hardly anything you're thinking anymore. It don't matter if it's me, I guess, but it ain't good to hold things in. If you read the Willie Nelson book, you'd know that. He always says that.'

'I could tell you, I guess,' I said.

'About Annie?'

'Yeah,' I said. And then I told him. About that night, the night I went down to the Sutro and saw her like that, with that guy. With her naked down to her bottom underwear, with her bare knees on that old carpet, with her mom naked in the same room.

When I finished I took a drink off the whiskey and got another beer. I couldn't even look him in the eyes.

'She's lived a hard life,' Jerry Lee said after a long pause. 'Her mom's a hooker, for Christsakes.'

'I know,' I said.

'Maybe she's all right, maybe she had to do it like she said. It's hard to think of it any other way. I guess, in the end, we don't know what kind of things she's had to put up with. But you remember that time she came with her face all bloody. Her eyes black and blue.'

'Yeah,' I said.

'Her mom beat the shit out of her. Or the time her mom took all the money she'd saved to buy a car. Stole it from her. Or when her mom burned her with the curling iron. You've seen her legs.'

'I know all that,' I said, staring at the ground.

'Look, if you came home one night and she was getting it on

196

with Al or Tommy, that would be one thing, but she wasn't like that. She didn't flirt with no one but you. I saw, hell, I saw her all the time. She sure as hell never flirted with me. You know she might be right, she might of had to do it, for her mom I mean. I'd probably bet money it ran that way. So I'd give her another chance. I think she's good. She might fuck up, but she's good underneath, I got a feeling on that.

'We're fuck ups, Frank, so we're gonna be with people that are fuck ups. And to me, to me, that makes sense. But that doesn't make them bad people, does it? If you've had bad luck, it doesn't mean you'll always have bad luck, does it? Some people that are unlucky, they can get lucky. Not everyone's cursed, I don't think. And you need someone. Of any guy in the whole world you do. You're the loneliest guy I know. Everyone says that. Even Tommy says that.'

'When I saw her,' I said and finally looked at him, 'I did feel better. Like I could be better.'

'Sometimes it's hard, man. You got to take a risk.'

'Maybe,' I said and threw my empty beer into the small basket by the TV.

'I made you something,' Jerry Lee said and picked up his drawing pad. 'I drew this for you,' he said and handed it to me.

It was of me and him and the dog. We were driving in our new car and Jerry Lee was at the wheel, the dog was in the middle and I was in the passenger seat. On the roof of the car were cans of beer, and above all that was a banner that read 'The Flannigan Brothers' and below that 'The three high rolling hard going travelers.'

'That's funnier than hell,' I said and laughed.

197

'It's all right,' he said and then paused for a time. 'But you know what I've been thinking about, well, it's just that . . . that I ain't done anything yet. I ain't done anything great or memorable or done anything that's helped anyone else.'

'Don't say that.'

'It's true,' he said. 'I haven't done anything. I've never even had a girl tell me she's loved me. You have, haven't you? Hasn't Annie told you that?'

'Yeah,' I said.

'All I've done is fuck up. At least the last few years, anyway. I'm not complaining, really, and I don't want you to tell me it ain't true. It's the facts the way I see them and that's what I mean. I'm just trying to be honest. I've never really done anything. I didn't even graduate from high school, and everyone can do that. Only real bums don't. And I've never had a real girlfriend, someone that was just mine. Polly always had another boyfriend. Always. She never once stopped with just me. We never really talked about anything or gave each other presents at Christmas. I never took her out to dinner or went away with her like when you took Annie to San Francisco on the goddamn Amtrak train. I don't know, now I got you in trouble, and I killed the kid, Wes Denny. It was me, I did that. Whether or not it was my fault doesn't matter, it happened, and it happened to me. 'Cause I'm here. 'Cause I'm alive in the world that poor kid's dead.'

'You're just getting started. Our lives, we got a lot of years.'

'No girl's gonna fuck a guy with no leg. A guy who's killed a kid.'

I opened another beer and took another long pull off the whiskey.

'This is a depressing conversation.'

'I'm just telling the truth,' Jerry Lee said.

'I don't think so,' I said. I went over to the cassette player, flipped the tape and turned up the song 'Railroad Lady'. We didn't talk for a long time.

'Tell me a story,' Jerry asked when the tape ended. You could hear the wind howl around us, shaking the old dilapidated motel.

'Hell, I don't feel like it,' I said. 'I'm drunker than hell, and all I want to do is pass out and not think anymore.'

'Shit, Frank, I ain't gonna sleep, I never sleep when I've had a few. I gave you the drawing, you owe me. Like we used to be. This might be the last time we get to sit like this for a long time. I mean, if I go to the hospital tomorrow this might be it. So tell me one.'

'What do you want to hear?'

'Well, I want to hear one about me, I guess. Something good, where I get married or at least get a girl. Maybe I'm famous or something. You could make me rich, if you want.'

'All right,' I said and thought for a while. 'Well, I guess I could start here. It was World War Two, and you and me were pilots, fighter pilots, and we were stationed in England. We were heading over to Germany one morning when we ran into a bunch of German fighter planes and we got into a huge dogfight. "Tiger one, I'm hit," yelled Pete Harris from Ohio, one of our good buddies. He went into a spin and crashed into the ocean, the English Channel. Martin, Lewis, Johnson, they all got hit and spun in circles and crashed into the freezing sea. We were taking out Jerry, though, one by one we were. Soon it was down to Captain Wilson, me, and you. Then you got hit, you had a Nazi on your tail, and I came zipping up behind you and I blew the bastard up. "Thanks,

Tiger five," you said over the radio. The rest of the Germans ran, headed back over the Channel. Problem was, your plane was out of control. Set northwest with a broken rudder, you couldn't steer. You were heading towards Iceland, Greenland, and there was nothing you could do about it. Captain Wilson, he was hit, his arm got blown off and he was heading back to base. Me, I followed you for a time.

'"Tiger five," you said, "I don't have control, heading into cloud cover, ideas at a minimum."

'Jesus, I didn't know what to do. I stayed behind you, but my gas tank had been hit. Gas was spewing out, my engine started smoking. "Tiger four, I'm leaking fuel, going to have to pull out and head back to base. When you find land, parachute out. We'll regroup. You get to a radio and contact base control and we'll do a recon-mission into wherever you're at and pick you up. Head towards Amsterdam, over and out."

'"Tiger five, I copy that. Good luck, kill those Jerries for me, I'll do the same. Happy hunting, over and out."

'Well, I saw your plane disappear into cloud cover and I limped my way back to England. It was rough going, I had to climb up as high as I could in order to coast down. I was on fumes by the time I saw the runway. Captain Wilson had already landed. He was drinking English tea and smoking a cigar while they sewed his goddamn arm back on. I landed all right, and I jumped out of the plane and yelled, "Get me a goddamn fighter, my brother's up there, controls locked, I'm gonna do a mid-air transfer."

'Wilson coughed, "No one can do a mid-air transfer. That hasn't been done since the great Waldo Pepper did it in World War One."

'"Get me a plane, I can do it, captain."

'"I bet you can, you crazy bastard, get this soldier a goddamn plane!"

'"All our planes are too shot up," the head mechanic, Roscoe, yelled out.

'"Don't know what to tell you, kid," Captain Wilson said, then passed out. In the meantime you were heading out into the Atlantic, right towards Iceland. You kept the plane up, but it was hard. "I got to hold on," you said over and over. "Got to get back and kill more Jerries." And you did hold on all the way to Iceland, where it's the middle of winter and snowing like a son of a bitch. Once you see land you bail out, hit your parachute jump cord, and sail down to a goddamn blizzard. You walk for miles.'

I paused and opened a new beer.

'This is a good one,' Jerry Lee said. 'Action and adventure. Keep it going.'

'I'm not quite done yet. Almost, though,' I continued. 'So you walk for miles. You can barely see, it's a whiteout and you're almost snow blind when you see a polar bear the size of an elephant and it starts chasing you, trying to eat you. You pull out your pearl-handled forty-five and with one shot you hit it in the head, right through the brain, and kill it. But you're fucking cold, frozen almost, so you take out your Air Force issue pocket knife and cut a hole in the polar bear and jump inside it to keep warm.'

'That's fucking sick,' Jerry Lee said and laughed.

'Yeah, but it saved your life, and in the morning the sun came out and you jumped out and started walking again. For miles you walked, covered in polar-bear blood and guts that began to freeze on you as the wind kicked in. Then finally, after almost falling into

201

a frozen lake, you see a house, a cabin, you see smoke coming from its chimney. Well, you beat on the door, but no one answers and so you just walk in. You can hear someone screaming, a girl, but you can't see where. The cabin's small, just a table with a white cloth on it, some chairs, and a fireplace with a fire going. There's something cooking, an apple pie, in a stove. But there's a back room and you don't know what to do. You keep hearing the screaming and then the crying, and so you walk into the room and there before you is a guy around fifty years old and he's got this girl tied face down on the bed naked. Goddamn if he isn't doing cocaine off the girl's ass. And the girl, she's maybe twenty, dark hair, beautiful. She's got whip marks on her back and the guy, the fat, hairy, smelly guy dressed in a red one-piece long johns outfit, snorts a huge line, the size of a deer's antler, off her right ass cheek and then he whips her and yells at her in Icelandic. The girl lets out a scream and then you say, "Sir, I'm a lieutenant in the American Air Force stationed in England. Sir, put down that whip." The guy he looks over and sees you, and he's scared, you look like the devil with all the polar-bear blood on you. You pull your gun out and make the guy lay down on the floor and then you untie the girl. She grabs you and thanks you in English, then runs into the kitchen, naked, and she's the best looking girl you've ever seen. You let her go 'cause you still have your eye on the guy, and she comes running back with a big kitchen knife and stabs the guy in the throat and blood comes shooting out in a stream and hits the wall.'

'This is a good one,' Jerry Lee says, laughing.

'Well, the guy he turns out to be her father, and he's laying there dying, and she begins crying and you're not sure what to do, and

202

then finally the guy dies and she gets dressed. Both of you drag the man out into the snow and soon a pack of wolves come and they eat him and drag his bones away. Then the girl, the girl who's smart as hell and knows English just from listening to the radio, helps you undress and takes you to an outdoor tub they have that is a hot spring and you jump in there, and then she jumps in too. She screams 'cause of the whip marks on her back, but she gets used to it. Then she tells you about her cocaine-addicted father, her isolation out there, the polar bear that ate her sister and her mother. You then tell her about your life as a fighter pilot, your plane that you couldn't steer, your night in the guts of the polar bear, and your twenty-mile hike to the cabin.

'All night long you two keep talking, and she's funnier than hell. The next day she washes your clothes and feeds you seal steaks and apple pie and coffee. For weeks a blizzard ensues and all you can do is sit in the tub and eat her good food and talk to her. You've never been able to talk to anyone the way you do with her. You end up falling in love, she tells you you're the greatest man she's ever met. She wakes you up one night and crawls in bed with you naked and for the next month you stay there in that bed. Eating and fucking, fucking and eating. Then as the storm finally breaks you snowshoe into town, and you get married to her. And in celebration you go to the local tavern and you're getting loaded with her when on the radio you hear news that the war's over, that we killed the Jerries and soon the Japs will be done too. You and your wife, you go back to the cabin for your honeymoon, and you're laying out there in the hot spring and she's sitting on top of you talking to you in her Icelandic accent and she's happier than hell, and you're happier than hell, and then a goddamn meteor comes flying out of the sky and hits a half-mile from the cabin.

'"That is most beautiful thing I see," she says in her broken English.

'You both get dressed in your brand new polar bear winter suits that you got as a wedding present and you snowshoe out to the meteor and Jesus Christ if there isn't oil shooting a hundred yards into the sky.

'"Honey," you ask her, "you own this land?"

'"We own this land," she says and hugs you.

'"We're gonna be millionaires," you say as you watch the shooting crude.

'"I not care, I got you," she says.

'"Goddamn," you say and look at her Icelandic face and kiss her.

'The end,' I say and take a long drink off my beer.

'That's a good one,' Jerry Lee says and laughs. 'Maybe the best ever. What's her name?'

'Maybe it's Marge's long-lost sister Helen, her sister that got stranded in that near catastrophic shipwreck,' I said.

When I woke the next morning Jerry Lee was already awake. I looked over and his face had a film of sweat on it. He was as pale as I'd ever seen him.

'I think there's really something wrong with my leg,' he said. 'I ain't sure, but I think there's a smell to it, and it doesn't smell like anything I've smelled before.'

'Let me see,' I said and got up. I went over to him and pulled back the covers and even from there, where I stood, I could smell something foul, something not right.

'Jesus,' I said. 'It didn't smell like that earlier, did it?'

'No, not like that,' Jerry Lee said worriedly.

'We got to go to the hospital.'

'I don't want to go to jail,' Jerry Lee said.

'You won't go to jail, and even if you do, it probably won't be for that long.'

'I can't even hardly raise my arms today, either. You don't think I'm gonna die, do you?' he said and looked at me. Tears began leaking down his face. 'I guess maybe we should go to the hospital.'

'Don't worry, you're going to be all right,' I said and got dressed and helped him into some clothes. I carried him out to the car, and as I did I could feel how much weight he'd lost.

There was snow on the ground, but the roads were okay, and we didn't say anything on the ride over, but as I parked the car in the hospital lot he said, 'Is it wrong for me to want to live even though I killed that kid?'

'No,' I told him.

'I want to fall in love and have someone fall in love with me,' he said quietly. Then he cried so hard you could barely understand him. 'Do you think that's wrong to want? I mean, after what's happened?'

'No,' I said.

I put him in the wheelchair and pushed him up the ramp and into the main lobby. The nurses came then and took him. I waited for days and I sat with him as I had before, but each time I came he was worse. He would barely talk and just slept most of the time. They had to do another surgery to remove the infected part of his hurt leg, and when they did that, he died. He was in that hospital for just over a week, and then he was gone. I remember the day they told me, and I left that horrible building with nothing but a bag of his things. They asked me what I wanted to do with his body and things like that, and I told them that I'd need a day or so to think about it. But I knew that I'd never go back there, that his body and where it ended up didn't matter to me anymore. With my mother we'd had a funeral and a wake, and neither of those things had meant anything to me. She was just gone, and now my brother was too.

I remember after they gave me the news I sat there for a long time outside that old hospital. There were people coming in and going out, and I guess that's just the way of things.

Then I walked around, me and the dog did. Up and down the streets of that small town. I'd look in windows, but there was no reason to it. I didn't know what else to do. In the end I just waited outside the hardware store where Annie James worked. I hoped. Because hope, it's better than having nothing at all.

Written by Frank Flannigan December 10–29 at the Terrace Park Apartment Building, Elko, Nevada.
Drawings and sketches by Jerry Lee Flannigan.